# MYSTERY ON THE MISSISSIPPI

# Your TRIXIE BELDEN Library

# Trixie Belden and the
# MYSTERY ON THE MISSISSIPPI

BY KATHRYN KENNY

## Cover by Jack Wacker

GOLDEN PRESS
Western Publishing Company, Inc.
Racine, Wisconsin

# CONTENTS

# MYSTERY ON THE MISSISSIPPI

# Promise of Adventure • 1

THE DOOR of the Bob-White clubhouse burst open, and Trixie Belden, fourteen, rushed in. Her cheeks were flushed, her sandy curls in disarray, and her big blue eyes round with excitement. Honey Wheeler, her best friend, followed close behind her.

"Guess what!" Trixie called to the club members inside.

"A black bear is right on your heels!" her brother Mart said, and, in mock fear, he slammed the door through which the girls had just entered.

Trixie dropped into a chair, pulled Honey into the

one next to her, and sat gasping and laughing. "Mart, it's a thousand times more exciting than that. You couldn't ever guess in a hundred years!"

"They've discovered a large quantity of oil in our flower garden."

"Guess again. You're not even warm."

"There's gold in them thar hills back of the Wheelers' game preserve," Mart suggested.

"No, but you're getting nearer. It does have something to do with Honey's father."

"Something to do with Dad?" Honey's older brother, Jim, called from a corner of the big clubhouse room. "How come? Dad was just leaving for the commuter train when I came over here. What is it, Trixie?"

"If you'll give me one little minute, I'll tell you . . . but then, maybe I'd better wait till the others get here. . . ."

Mart jumped to his feet in protest. "Trixie Belden, you know you'll never be able to hold out till *all* the Bob-Whites are together. Dan won't get away from his job till evening, and Diana won't even be back home for a month. Five of the seven Bob-Whites are here. That's a quorum or whatever you call it. Come on, Trixie, out with it before you pop!"

"Well, then, here it is," Trixie said slowly and importantly. "How'd you like to fly to St. Louis, Missouri—right to the place where the spaceships are made—where the factories are right *at* the airport, practically. . . ."

"Golly . . . neat! Is it on the level, Trix?" Mart asked excitedly.

Trixie, her eyes dancing, nodded emphatically. "Mr. Wheeler has some business in St. Louis with one of the biggest aircraft manufacturers in the world!"

"So what?" her oldest brother, Brian asked. "He often does that. That's not news."

"Well, *this* is! One of the executives flew here yesterday to talk to Honey and Jim's father. He came in a big private plane. He's going to fly back tomorrow, take Mr. Wheeler with him, and—"

"Take some of us along? Who? Which ones? Me?" Mart shouted.

"Not some of us. All of us! Every one of the Bob-Whites," Honey said, then added soberly, "except Diana, 'cause she's away, and maybe Dan can't leave his job to go—but isn't it exciting?"

"I'll say!" Mart grabbed his cap. "I've *got* to go tell Dan. He's coaching those Little Leaguers today. Maybe the Park Board will let him take time off to go with us. Jeepers! On-the-spot inspection of a capsule that may go to the moon!" He disappeared through the door.

"If he'd waited just a minute, I could have told him one thing," Jim said seriously. "He should know it himself. All that spacecraft business is classified. We won't get within a mile of one of the factories."

"Yes, we will, Jim," Trixie insisted. "Won't we, Honey?"

"Daddy did say, Jim, that there's an exhibit there that'll be open to the public. We can at least see a capsule that carried one of the astronauts into orbit."

"Don't you think we can see anything of the space program?" Jim insisted. "I wish I'd had a chance to talk to Dad."

"You can ask him this evening when he gets home from the city. There's room on the plane for ten people—ten passengers, I mean, in addition to the crew. There'll be only six of us, and that's counting Dan. We have to be ready to leave, though, sometime tomorrow."

"I can leave right now!" Brian said, his usually quiet voice loud with excitement. "Say—there's lots more to St. Louis than just spaceships. Have you stopped to think that it's on the Mississippi River? We could maybe take a steamboat to Hannibal; you know, right in Huck Finn and Tom Sawyer country. Or even to New Orleans. . . ."

"Wait a minute, Brian. We aren't going to be there the rest of the summer, you know. How long did Dad say we'd be gone, Honey?" Jim asked his sister quickly.

"Less than a week," Honey murmured.

"Good-bye, New Orleans!" Brian said sadly. "Oh,

well, I'll settle for Hannibal or any other place on the river, in a steamboat!"

"Me, too. I'm so excited I'm about to explode!" Trixie took hold of Brian's arm. "We'd better go break the news to Moms."

Trixie and Brian hurried down the hill to Crabapple Farm, which sprawled in simple, cozy comfort in the valley of the Catskills. A white picket fence spread its arms to enclose Mrs. Belden's rose beds, an apple orchard, and the kitchen garden. Mr. Belden worked at the bank in the village, Sleepyside-on-the-Hudson, and Mrs. Belden was . . . well, she was just "Moms" to Brian, Mart, Trixie, and little Bobby . . . oh, yes, and to Reddy, their Irish setter.

On a rising slope above Crabapple Farm, the Wheeler home stood, surrounded by riding stables, a lake for swimming and skating, and a huge game preserve.

Brian and Jim, seniors at Sleepyside Junior-Senior High, and Trixie, Honey, and Mart were the original members of the club, the Bob-Whites of the Glen. The old Wheeler gatehouse was their beloved clubhouse. The Bob-Whites had pitched in with muscle, paint, and plaster, and now the house was sturdy and weathertight and attractively decorated inside. When Diana Lynch, Trixie's age, had moved into a big house near the Wheelers, seeming lonesome and lost, the Bob-Whites had invited her to join their club. Later on, Dan Mangan, the orphaned nephew of Regan, the Wheelers' stableman, became the seventh member.

The Bob-Whites were a close-knit, loyal group, who worked together on many worthwhile projects to gather funds for UNICEF, Red Cross, and local and national relief needs. All of these endeavors had a way of turning into fantastic, oftentimes downright dangerous, adventures.

Trixie seemed to have a sixth sense that had often helped confused law officers to solve puzzling cases. When the Bob-Whites had been on vacation together, she and Honey had investigated mysteries on an Arizona dude ranch, a sheep farm in Iowa, a cabin in the Missouri Ozarks, in New York City, and even in their own small village of Sleepyside. With Honey, her valuable aide, Trixie expected someday to operate the Belden-Wheeler Detective Agency.

Just as they worked faithfully together, the Bob-Whites enjoyed good times most when they were together, especially since wherever Trixie went, there was bound to be excitement. "Trixie draws crooks to her like a magnet," Mart once said. "She can spot one quicker'n a bloodhound." It was no wonder, then, that they were fascinated with the possibilities of the promised plane trip to St. Louis.

They didn't dream, though, as they packed for their journey, of the many dangers they would face before returning to their clubhouse at home.

As it turned out, Dan was able to go along on the trip, for a substitute took over his work. Diana, vacationing with her family, was the only Bob-White missing as they checked in at the Vacation Inn near the Lambert-St. Louis airport.

"I guess all the Bob-Whites had better get rooms close together," Jim told his father as the registration clerk offered him a pen.

"You're right; you'd better stick together," his father answered. He would take a room down the hall but would spend much of his time at the home of the airplane executive, Mr. Brandio. "No one can predict what Trixie will be up to. You and the other boys must keep an eye on her. Mr. Brandio is going to let you have a car, Jim. The city is about an hour's drive from here. Trixie can't get far away unless you drive her."

"Trixie doesn't need to be watched, Daddy," Honey told him. "Neither do I."

"Of course not. I was only fooling. No, I wasn't fooling altogether. Trixie has been in some pretty dangerous situations. Let's have this trip be only fun. Right, Trixie?" He smiled at her warmly.

"I *never* hunt for cases," Trixie insisted. "Can I help it if there are times when Honey and I just have to step in and help solve a mystery?"

"I guess not," Mr. Wheeler answered soberly. "I

guess not. I can't help it, either, Trixie, if I'm relieved to know that you will all be quartered near to one another. Have fun, now! The car is parked in the back parking lot, Jim. Here's the key. I'll be in touch with you."

Mart caught up the key and passed it on to Jim. "How do we get from here to Mr. Brandio's factory, sir?"

"What for?" Mr. Wheeler asked.

"To see some of the space stuff. You know, one of the capsules that orbited the earth . . . maybe the one that's going to the moon. . . ."

"Are you serious, Mart?"

"I sure am. What's wrong?"

"It's classified, that's what," Brian broke in. "We'd have told you that back at the clubhouse, if you hadn't gone hunting Dan so suddenly. All that business at the factories is classified. Isn't that so, Mr. Wheeler?"

"I'm afraid it is. There's an exhibit to be opened to the public later on. Say, I hope you're not terribly disappointed. There are lots of other things to see in St. Louis. With the car you can hunt them out—"

"Thanks, Mr. Wheeler," Trixie interrupted, frowning at Mart. "We'll find lots of good places to go. Don't you bother about us for one minute."

"That's good," Mr. Wheeler said, relieved, and hurried to where Mr. Brandio waited in his car.

The boys carried the luggage from the motel office down the wide walk that circled the pool. Children splashed there, calling delightedly to one another. Overhead, jet planes were taking off and landing. Taxicabs roared in to discharge passengers and to pick up others. Maids hurried about making rooms ready for new occupants.

"This is our room right here," Trixie told Jim, seeing the number on the door. He and Brian carried the girls' bags inside. "You two are just next to us, and Dan and Mart are on the other side of you. Isn't that right?"

"Right," Jim agreed. "Whistle when you're ready. We'll decide then what we'll do today."

Inside their room, Trixie put her bag on a luggage rack. "I'll just hang up my dresses. I don't think I'll need more than these two." She opened the closet door, then whistled. "Say, Honey, I don't believe the maid had quite finished getting this room ready. Someone must still be living here. At least, there's something on this shelf that looks like a briefcase. I guess we were too anxious to get into our room—or the maid thought we were."

Honey stood on tiptoe and looked around the closet. "There aren't any clothes here; nothing but that briefcase."

"I guess not. Maybe I'd better take it to the motel office. Some businessman must have left it. Heavens,

I hope he hasn't needed it. Of all the things to forget!"

Trixie reached up to the shelf, and the briefcase fell to the floor, spilling papers. "Jeepers! It wasn't zipped. Help me pick 'em up, please, Honey."

The girls squatted on the floor and hastily gathered the contents together. Trixie was aware only of some yellow sheets heavily scribbled with figures, and a medley of graph paper. She tried to stuff them into the bulging case. She was so absorbed in what she was doing that she didn't hear the door open. A gruff voice brought her, startled, to her feet. "Hand that over! It's mine, young ladies!"

An angry-faced, dark-haired stranger grabbed the case from her hands roughly. His piercing black eyes flashed fire. "What do you mean by opening my dispatch case?"

Trixie, alarmed by the man's fury, couldn't answer. She stood as though hypnotized. Honey, too, was surprised into speechlessness.

The man tried hastily to stuff the papers back into the case, glaring at the trembling girls. "Don't you know you shouldn't touch other people's property? What were you doing with my papers? Meddlers!" He gave Trixie a vicious nudge with his elbow.

Honey recovered her voice. "We didn't even touch your old papers!" she said coldly.

"And we'll thank you to take your belongings and get out of our room," Trixie added. "There!" She slammed the door so hard it shook.

Honey went to the window and watched the tall, foreign-looking man stride down the pool walk. "Of all the rude people! I hope he misses his taxi . . . misses his plane. I hope...."

"Oh, rats, who cares about him?" Trixie answered.

Honey turned from the window and laughed. "You do."

"I do not, Honey Wheeler. I just. . . . Well, what *did* make him act so mean? There must have been something odd in that briefcase."

"Yes. All those graphs were certainly strange. They had queer designs on them."

"Honey, this motel *is* right near all those airplane factories."

"He looked like a foreign agent, too!" Honey exclaimed. "Did you notice his eyes?"

"They'd bore a hole right through the walls. Golly, he almost hypnotized me."

"Me, too. Gosh, Trixie, do you suppose he could be a spy?"

"Who knows? He acted kind of strange, for sure. Say, do you suppose those papers over there in the wastebasket belonged to him? The maid evidently didn't empty it."

"Maybe they *are* his." Honey grasped the wastebasket and brought out a handful of crumpled papers. "Look at this!"

Trixie straightened them out on top of the dressing table. "Hmmm . . . more of that graph paper. He *could* have been copying plans. These sheets have figures all over them. And writing, too. There's a map of the Mississippi River, and look at these queer drawings along the river!"

"Let me see. They're not well drawn. Maybe he just sketched them for his children."

"I don't think so. I think they're much more important than that." Trixie folded the papers together and put them in her purse. "We'd better meet the boys and show them what we've found. Jim will know whether there's anything odd about them. Let's go, Honey."

"You'd better not tell Jim and Brian how that man shoved you with his elbow. They'd knock his block off."

"I thought that was what *you* were going to do," Trixie said. "You turned on him like a wildcat."

"I was scared—awfully scared, Trixie. I hope we never run into him again."

"I . . . just . . . think . . . we . . . may," Trixie said slowly and mysteriously. "I have one of my strange premonitions."

# Catfish Princess · 2

JIM, BRIAN, DAN, AND MART sat on a bench at the pool's edge, waiting for the girls.

"Golly, Trix," Dan said, "why do girls take so long to fix their faces or whatever they do? We could have been halfway to the city by this time."

"Wait *just* a second, Dan." Trixie fumbled in her purse and brought out the papers. "What do you think of these?" She leaned over the bench back and dropped the sheets in Jim's lap.

"What are they? Where did you get them?" he asked curiously.

Honey told him. ". . . and you should have seen the way he looked when he found us picking up the papers from the floor."

"He looked as though he could kill us!" Trixie said dramatically. "Do those papers look odd to you, Dan? Brian? Mart? What's the matter with you, Jim? What's so funny?"

"Nothing, Trix. Nothing." Jim smothered a grin. "I can't help laughing when I think that if Dad had waited just fifteen minutes longer, he'd have seen you put on your gumshoes and start sleuthing."

"I'm *not* sleuthing. I just wanted to show you this stuff and ask you what you think I should do with it."

"If you were asking me, I'd say to take it back and give it to the man you saw," Brian said.

Jim agreed. "I don't see any reason to be worked up over these papers. You'd better do as Brian suggested. Give 'em back."

Trixie frowned. "Do *you* think so, Dan?"

"I'm not too sure. I didn't see the man, and you and Honey did. You're usually right when you think something odd is going on."

"Don't let Brian and me influence you, Trix," Jim told her.

"I won't. Maybe I *should* just take them back. He's probably miles away by this time, though. He seemed to be in a hurry. Oh, well, forget it for now, anyway." Trixie put the papers back into her purse. "Let's get going to wherever you want to go."

"*We* want to try to get on the next steamboat that docks in St. Louis," Mart said.

"That sure won't be today. Things just don't work out that fast," Brian said. "Anyway, Trix, while we were waiting for you and Honey, we asked at the motel desk, and the man there didn't know anything about steamboats. He had some vague idea that there's one steamboat still cruising up and down the Mississippi. I asked him when it would stop at St. Louis, and he didn't know."

"He told us we could ask at the Jefferson Memorial in Forest Park," Jim added. "That's where they have all kinds of historical stuff—model rooms from old steamboats and other things about the river. I'd sort of like to go there this afternoon. We could explore the rest of Forest Park, too—the zoo and the model railroad. Dad told us all about the place when he came back from one of his trips here. Forest Park is supposed to be almost as exciting as Central Park in New York City. Do you have your camera, Trixie?"

Trixie's hand went to her mouth in dismay. "I forgot it. I was so confused by the way that man acted. I'll run and get it. I won't be a second."

Back at her room, Trixie found the door open. The maid was still working there. "I've almost finished now," she told Trixie. Then her voice fell to a whisper. "That man outside in the utility area wanted to get in here to see if he'd left anything. See him?"

The dark-haired man had his back to Trixie and was rifling through papers in a big trash basket. He turned, started to speak to her, then seemed to change his mind.

"What's he doing?" Trixie whispered quietly to the maid.

"Hunting for some papers I must have emptied from the basket in your room. That's what he told me. If you ask me, I think he's a little bit. . . ." She pointed to her temple and shook her head.

"Why?"

"He raised the roof when I said he couldn't go inside your room. He made such a fuss, I had to let him go in, but I went along, too, to see that he didn't touch any of your things. He's a queer one."

The man seemed to sense that they were talking about him. He looked at the maid viciously. Visibly frightened, she raised her voice to throw him off the track. "Where's the first place you're going sightseeing, Miss Belden?"

"We're all just crazy to take a ride on a steamboat," Trixie answered. "I guess we'll go to the Jefferson Memorial first, to see the exhibit of old steamboats there. Someone there surely will know about present traffic on the river."

"Sure they will. I'll be through here in just a few minutes."

Trixie hesitated at the door. *Maybe I'd better do exactly what Brian told me to do,* she thought. *Maybe I should give the papers back.* She started to open her purse, then reconsidered. *I think I'll just hold on to them for a while. A person doesn't get as angry as he did unless he's doing something shady. I'd like to know who he is. Guess I'll ask at the desk.*

As Trixie left, the man stood up, cursed under his breath, and said hoarsely to the maid, "Why did you have to wait around forever? Now it's too late."

Trixie wasn't quite sure she had understood what he had said. She stopped, perplexed, then went on to the desk.

In answer to her inquiry, the clerk pointed to the register. It read: "Pierre Lontard, General Delivery, New Orleans, Louisiana."

"Boy, did you take your time!" Mart greeted her. "The camera must have been buried in the bottom of a trunk."

Trixie paid no attention to him. "Guess what that man's name is," she said mysteriously.

"What man?" Brian asked.

"The one I told you about, the one who grabbed the briefcase in our room. His name is Pierre Lontard. He's from New Orleans!"

"So what?" Mart looked disgusted. "New Orleans is a big city, Trix. Boy, are you hard up for a mystery,

if you have to make something out of the fact that a
guy lives in New Orleans!"

"It isn't just that. He *is* mysterious. His address is
just 'General Delivery.' If a person can't give a street
address, there's something strange about him."

"Oh, for pete's sake, Trix, forget him!" Brian took
his sister's arm to hurry her on toward the parking lot.
"Give you a little time, and you'll come up with a
better mystery than that. Let's get the show on the
road."

"All right. You can make fun of me if you want
to. . . ."

"I'm not making fun of you, Trixie," Honey said
as she hurried to catch up. "There's that man now,
over there near our car. See him? He's the one just
getting into that black Mercedes. He's having some
trouble unlocking his car."

"I'm having some trouble myself," Jim said, "but
it's not with the lock. It's getting you girls into the
car and on the way. Crowd in. Here we go."

The car turned sharply and sped down the road
leading to the main highway.

Trixie, still skeptical, turned her head. "He's right
behind us now!" she exclaimed.

"Give him a run for his money!" Mart cried. Jim
stepped on the accelerator. At a stop sign, the big
black car crowded close. It seemed to be trying to
sideswipe the small car. Inside, the man bent to

watch for the light to change.

As the signal turned green, the Bob-Whites' car shot ahead into a free lane.

From the rear window, Trixie, Mart, and Honey watched the Mercedes as it disappeared behind a huge truck.

"I'll bet he's spitting fire!" Trixie cried exultantly.

"I'll bet a cookie he doesn't know we're alive," Mart insisted.

"We'll see. Just you wait and see. *Of course* he knows we're alive. You know what Mr. Wheeler told us. This whole area for miles around could just be alive with spies. Lots of people want to know what's going on in those airplane factories."

Mart exploded, laughing. "Do you think for a minute any spy would think a bunch of teen-age kids would know anything about plans our government might have?"

Trixie bristled. "Pierre Lontard *did* see us arriving with a big executive of one of the companies, didn't he? That is, he could have seen us, if he'd wanted to. *I* think he wanted to, so there!"

"I do, too," Honey said loyally, "else why did he act so funny about those papers in his briefcase?"

"She has something there," Jim told the other boys soberly. "You have to admit that."

Mart was unconvinced. "All coincidence. Simply just happened. Let's skip Trix and her suspicions for a while. That's the Memorial over there, where you turn off of Lindell Boulevard, isn't it, Jim?"

Jim rounded the curve when the light changed, then headed the car into a parking space. "Everybody out!" he ordered.

"Let's stop at the office first," Brian suggested. "Maybe we can find out when the next steamboat leaves from the waterfront."

"Two bits says it'll be tomorrow!" Mart shouted hopefully. "Brian, you ask. There's the office."

They crowded around the desk, and they all spoke at once. Just past them lay the glamorous steamboat room.

"Whoa! Whoa! Slow down there! One at a time," the gray-haired man at the desk said with a smile. "What's that? Next steamboat? What one are you talking about? There's only one left on the Mississippi that takes trips of any consequence. She's the *Delta Queen.*"

"That's our boat!" Mart shouted. "When does she depart?"

"A couple of months from now."

"What?" the Bob-Whites chorused.

"I said a couple of months from now—more or less. She only makes one trip a year. She leaves Cincinnati and runs down the Ohio to Cairo, Illinois, around two hundred miles south of here. That's where the Ohio joins the Mississippi. Then she goes on to New

Orleans and back up the river to St. Paul. She stops here going and coming—only twice a year."

"And we've missed her?" Trixie asked. The faces of the Bob-Whites fell in discouragement. "Not another steamboat of any kind?"

"Not a single one. There's an old one going to pieces down at the wharf. You can go and see her. There's another one made into a showboat. You can see a melodrama aboard her any night in the week."

"Not anything that travels on the river?" Jim asked.

"There's the *Admiral*. It's an excursion boat. It's nothing like an old-time steamboat. It's just for dancing and picnicking. Only cruises around about a ten-mile circle. She leaves several times a day."

"Not that!" Mart said in disgust. "Come on, gang. We can at least go and see what real steamboats *used* to look like."

The huge exhibit included authentic reproductions of several steamboat rooms typical of those on the mammoth paddle-wheelers found on the Mississippi a century before.

The pilothouse stood several steps above the floor, its huge wheel more than a man's height in diameter. In a tall chair, a dummy pilot sat gazing through the glass window. At his side, a bench sprawled—just such a bench as the cub pilot Samuel Clemens occupied as he watched his hero swing the big wheel to outguess the hazardous, swirling current.

"Golly!" Mart exclaimed. "It's no wonder a guy wanted to be a pilot in those days. It's really neat! Look at the murals all around us. Seems almost like being *on* the river!"

"If you think it seems real over there in the pilot-house, just come over here." Trixie beckoned from where she and Honey stood, hands tightly clasped, noses pressed against the glass windows of the lady's lounge. "Heavens, it's all red velvet! Look at that chandelier! Crystal and spangles and paintings and—"

"I'm liable to bust right open and die if we don't get to take some kind of a ride on that river!" Jim spoke with real feeling.

"It'll have to be the excursion boat *Admiral,* then," Trixie said sadly.

"I'll *never* settle for that. There must be something else. If we can get Dan away from that display of old guns up there on the balcony, we can go and ask that man at the office again. Dan!" Jim's voice echoed through the big room.

"Let him stay there. The rest of us can go ask," Mart said. "You'll never get a future New York policeman away from Kentucky rifles and dueling pistols. Right through this arch, Jim; there's the office. I don't know what earthly good it'll do to ask again. I can't stand it, though, if we don't get on that river somehow!"

"Hi, there!" the man back of the desk called as the Bob-Whites crowded through the door. "I've been keeping my eye out for you. There *is* a chance you can go on the river."

"No kidding?" Trixie asked. "On a real steamboat?"

"Did they rustle up an extra?" Mart asked.

"No steamboat. No extra. Something else, though. I don't know why I didn't think of it myself. A man was in here shortly after you left, and he reminded me of it."

"For heaven's sake, tell us!" Trixie insisted.

"I'm trying to, honey," the old gentleman said. "This man—he wanted to know if I could tell him where he could *buy* a steamboat—"

"And you knew, and you told him, and he said we could take a ride—" Trixie burst out.

"Hey, not so fast. Not so fast. No, sirree, but he did want to buy a steamboat. There's some of them tied up and rotting here and there between St. Louis and New Orleans—north on the river, too, for that matter. Yes, sir, though I doubt if any of them would float. He wants to make one of them watertight, float it down to New Orleans, use it for a showboat, and—"

"For pete's sake, how does that get us on the river?" Mart cried, forgetting his manners.

"I'm coming to that right now, if you'll just listen. Towboat. That's the answer. Think you'd like to take a trip down the river on one of them?"

"A towboat? You mean a tugboat?" Trixie's eyes were wide with wonder, remembering the puffing little harbor boats that are used to swing huge ocean liners into the channel.

"No, I don't mean a tugboat. I mean a towboat. There's a mighty big difference. It *pushes* barges. It doesn't *pull* them."

"I'd just as soon paddle an old scow," Brian said sadly. "What we wanted to do was to *live* on a steamboat for at least a couple of days."

"You can do that," the man answered. "At least, you *may* be able to. It's a matter of invitation. Towboats don't take passengers, but they *do* take guests. This man said there's one, the *Catfish Princess*, due to head south in a day or two. He seemed certain you could get aboard her."

"Are there living quarters on a towboat?" Trixie wanted to know.

"I'll say there are—as fine as any you'll find on an ocean liner. Well, maybe that's talking them up a little too much, but they're clean and neat. Food's good, too. Extra good. That's what the deckhands look forward to mostly—food. The towboats are actually run in much the same spirit as the old steamboats. The captains and pilots have wanted to be captains and pilots from the time they were little—"

"Holy cow!" Mart said and jumped into the air.

"What are we waiting for?"

"A little information about how to get on board," Jim answered quietly.

"Whom do you know in the city?" the man asked.

Dismayed, the Bob-Whites looked from one to another.

"Mr. Brandio!" Honey exclaimed suddenly.

"Don't know the name," the man replied. "Who is he?"

"The president, I think," Mart began. The man raised his eyebrows. "President of the Clear Meadow Aircraft Corporation, I mean. . . ."

The man whistled. "Well! *He* should be able to get you aboard. A man like that would have his hands in half a dozen enterprises. Ask him, anyway. By the way, that dark-haired man who just looked in here is the one trying to buy a steamboat. He's the one who made me think of a towboat for your trip. Hope you can make it. Come back and see us again."

"Thank you, sir, we surely will be back!" Jim said politely. "It's a swell place you have here!"

Outside, Trixie pointed over to the parking lot. "There he is, the man we saw at the motel, just getting into that Mercedes! It's the same man."

"Yeah." Mart put his two fingers to his head in a salute. "I don't think much of your manners on the highway, fella, but thanks for the tip about the *Catfish Princess!*"

# Good News • 3

As THE CAR SPED through the city to Lindbergh Boulevard, the road leading to the airport, Dan was very
quiet.

"Take a look back of you, Dan," Jim said over his
shoulder. "Do you see anything of our friend in the
Mercedes?"

Dan didn't answer.

"What's biting you?" Mart asked, concern shad-
owing his face.

"That bozo from New Orleans." Dan's face was
red. "Maybe he did give us a good steer about the

river, but why do you suppose he nearly wrecked us on the way into the city?"

Mart leaned forward to gaze at Dan. "Boy, are you slow to burn! Why didn't you say anything about that before?"

"I've just been doing a little thinking. It wasn't just happenstance, either, that took him to the Jefferson Memorial. I don't like the whole business."

Jim laughed. "Do you want to join the Belden-Wheeler Detective Agency, Dan? Didn't you ever have anyone try to crowd you out of a traffic lane before?"

"Sure. But why does he keep popping up all the time?"

"It's my guess we've seen the last of him," Jim said. "You forget that he was checking *out* of the motel when we checked in. That means he won't be around Vacation Inn, at least."

"He *wasn't* checking out," Trixie interrupted. "When I found out about his name, he was just changing to another room. He said it was too noisy by the pool. The clerk told me that because he wanted to know if I thought it would be too noisy for us."

"*Now* you tell us," Jim said patiently. "Say, Trixie, how about, from now on, our minding our own business and letting the Frenchman from New Orleans mind his?"

Dan still looked puzzled. "Then you don't think,

Jim, that he followed us to Jefferson Memorial?"

"For cat's sake, no. The man there told us he wanted to see if he could buy an old steamboat, didn't he?"

Dan's face colored. "Yeah, he did. I forgot about that, I guess. Count me out of your detective agency, Trixie."

"No, sirree! We need your help, Honey and I do. What would we have done without you when those jewel thieves kidnapped me in New York? You just keep on helping, Dan. Maybe Jim and Brian and Mart think there's nothing mysterious about Mr. Pierre Lontard, but I'm going to keep my eyes open, just the same."

"You do that, Trix," Jim told her. "In the meantime, I'll keep *my* eyes on this traffic. Did you ever see anything like it?"

"It's all going back and forth to those airplane factories." Trixie's face was very thoughtful. "That Lontard man will need a lot of watching, Honey."

Honey, wedged in between Jim and Brian in the front seat, nodded emphatically. "I'll help you all I can. You know that. Only, honestly, Trixie, I can't see anything very suspicious yet."

"You didn't look very closely at those odd papers in that briefcase, then, if you didn't see anything that was suspicious."

"I didn't. Neither did you. You didn't have any

more idea of what you were looking at than I did. You don't know what those papers in your purse are all about, either. I still think he may have been sketching and writing for his children."

"Dig out the papers, Trix," Dan suggested. "Let me have a good look at them."

"They're covered with figures. Scraggly lines, too, on the graph paper. Here they are, Dan. There are some words there that look Spanish. Honey, you know Spanish."

Dan smoothed out the crumpled papers. "Hmmmm . . . Spanish words. Sure, Honey knows some Spanish. Remember how she translated parts of that Mexican fortune-teller's prophecy?"

"Indeed I do remember!" Trixie took the papers from Dan. "Here they are, Honey. What are these words?"

"Move over a little, Brian," Honey said. "I can't see well. The writing is small and foreign-looking. Gosh, Trixie, it doesn't really look like Spanish. Yes, I guess it is. It's a kind of dialect, though, not the kind of Spanish I learned at boarding school."

"Can't you even recognize a word?" Dan asked impatiently.

"Give her time!" Brian said. "Keep your shirt on, Dan. How about it, Honey? See anything you know?"

"There's *dinero*. That means money. And . . . let me see . . . it says here *esté puntual*. . . ."

"Now we're getting someplace," Trixie said excitedly. "What does *esté puntual* mean?"

"Be on time."

"There you are! What more could you ask?" Trixie clapped her hands delightedly. "Those scraggly lines are copies of plans. They mean something aeronautical, as sure as you're born. And 'money' and 'be on time'— That couldn't mean anything but that he stole the plans, and he's going to get money for them, and he wants the money when it was promised!"

"Whoa! Back up a little!" Jim advised. He slowed the car and moved over to an outside lane. "Have another look at the paper. I doubt if anyone in South America is going to steal our country's plans. The South Americans are our allies."

Trixie shook her curls indignantly. "You forget, Jim, that people speak Spanish in Cuba. They'd give a lot of *dinero* to find out our space plans and pass them on to—"

Honey whooped. "You're right, Trixie. Right, as usual. See . . . here it says *La Habana* and . . . ohoooo . . . here it says *vamos a Cuba. . . .*"

"That doesn't sound much like writing for children," Mart said, puzzled. "Where'd you get that notion, Honey?"

"From the map of the river with those strange sketches. Show him that paper, Trixie."

Trixie straightened out the long narrow paper with

the outline of the Mississippi River. "I can't get much sense out of this," she said. "Can you?"

The crooked Mississippi meandered from the bottom of the sheet to the opposite corner at the top. Here and there along its course little drawings stood out.

"This looks like a fez," Mart said, pointing, "and here's a pyramid, and another. Heck, what could that be?"

"Egypt, of course," Brian said. "But what does Egypt have to do with spaceships? Here's something else funny—a set of false teeth. See, right in a row, and close by them, an island in the river."

"It looks like one of those picture puzzles in the bound copies of the old magazines we have in our school library," Honey said. "Rebuses, I think they called them."

"They really do," Trixie said, delighted with the interest the other Bob-Whites were showing. "I think this is the biggest puzzle of all—this picture of an old gray-bearded man, then a line of arrows pointing to an old steamboat."

"Yes, how about that?" Honey asked, awed.

"What are you going to do with this junk?" Dan asked. "As far as I can see, it's a lot of gobbledygook. What's your next move?"

"Show the papers to Mr. Brandio, of course," Honey said, "and to Daddy. Isn't that true, Trixie?"

Trixie folded the papers and put them back in her purse. "I don't think so," she said slowly. "We'd better wait awhile for that, Honey. I want to know more about this—and more about Mr. Lontard—before I run to your father and Mr. Brandio. They'd just laugh at me."

"Come to think of it, you're dead right," Mart said. "People from all over the world are in and out of Lambert-St. Louis airport. A few foreign words on scraps of paper can't mean much, Trix."

"Don't be too sure of that, Mart. I didn't mean I wasn't still suspicious. All I meant was that I want more to go on than I have now. More evidence is what I need. Honey and I'll have to find out if Pierre Lontard really is up to something shady. Then we'll take it up with the authorities."

"That sounds like sense," Brian said. "I suppose the FBI has a thousand rumors a day reported to them. I know you, though, Trix. You're just like a bulldog with a hold on a tramp's leg. You'll never let go. Forget it for now. Here's the motel, right ahead. Let's see what we can do about an invitation to go aboard the *Catfish Princess.* That's the first order of business. All agreed?"

"Right you are, Brian!" Jim said. He parked the car neatly, then glanced at his wristwatch. "It's about time to meet Dad for dinner. Let's hope he'll have some idea of how we can get on the towboat."

Mr. Wheeler *did* have an idea. "A lot of New York firms use Mississippi River barges to move freight," he said. "They're much cheaper than railroads for transporting freight . . . slower but dependable. You remember, Honey, when Mr. and Mrs. Thompson and their children visited us last summer?"

"Of course. I took the children swimming every day."

"That's right. Their father never has stopped saying what a wonderful baby-sitter you were."

"Thanks. What does that have to do with the *Catfish Princess?*"

"Possibly nothing at all. Mr. Thompson's firm does own a barge line on the Mississippi, though. Well, not exactly the Mississippi; his line starts back at Cincinnati."

"Do you think the Thompson firm might own the *Catfish Princess* or maybe some other towboat, Daddy, that would take guests?"

"I'll find out. I saw Mr. Thompson today at the Missouri Athletic Club, so I know he's in the city."

"Oh, will you call him? Right now?" Trixie's eyes were popping.

"Yes, Miss Now-or-Never, I will. I'll see if I can reach him. Go on into the dining room, and I'll stop at the phone booth over there. I'll join you later."

"Boy, are we ever lucky!" Mart said as they trooped into the dining room. "Seems as though all the Bob-Whites have to do is wish for something, and there it is!"

"We aren't on the towboat yet," Jim reminded him.

Trixie held up her crossed fingers. "Nothing, not a thing in this world, is going to keep us from taking that trip!"

Jim picked up the menu. "All I say is—just wait till we hear what Dad says. I know what I'm going to eat. Barbecued ribs, if they have them. There's Dad now. We'll soon know."

Mr. Wheeler started shaking his head before he reached the table. Trixie's spirits hit the floor with a thud. She pushed the menu away. "We're not going?" she asked Mr. Wheeler.

"Mr. Thompson sold his interest in the barge line several months ago. Hard luck, Bob-Whites."

"Doesn't he know someone who knows someone who could help us get aboard?" Jim asked. "Did you ask him that, Dad?"

"Of course I didn't. I waited for him to offer to do something more about it, and he didn't. He did tell me that barge lines almost never invite young people as guests. He said they were all over the place and got in all kinds of scrapes. Towboats aren't pleasure boats, of course."

"That's for sure," Brian agreed. "Didn't you tell him the Bob-Whites never mess around in what doesn't concern them?"

Mr. Wheeler took off his glasses, put them on the table in front of him, and smiled.

Jim joined in.

Then Brian.

Trixie looked puzzled.

"You don't see the joke, do you, Trix?" Mart asked. "Or you, either, Honey?"

"They all mean that we *do* mess around in what *they* think doesn't concern us," Honey answered. "I can think of some instances where they'd have been in a lot of trouble if we hadn't investigated things."

"You win there," Mr. Wheeler said. "I'm not giving up. When dinner's over, I'll give Mr. Brandio a ring and see if he can come up with an idea. Right now, let's order."

Mr. Brandio did not have an idea.

"His mind's so full of air travel that he doesn't know people still like to travel on water or land," Mr. Wheeler told the Bob-Whites.

Mart kissed his fingers into the air. "There goes a pipe dream!"

Honey sighed. "Oh, dear. Think *hard,* Daddy. You know so many people."

"I am thinking hard. The trouble with you, Honey, is that you think I'm a magician, that all I have to do to accomplish something is to wave a wand. . . ."

"You've waved a lot of wands for us Bob-Whites,

Mr. Wheeler," Trixie said gratefully. "Heavens, there are a lot of *other* things to do in St. Louis."

"Name one," Mart said disconsolately.

"I did so want to take just a little ride on the river. Daddy! You've thought of something!" Honey clapped her hands.

Mr. Wheeler had risen suddenly, snapping his fingers. He left abruptly, without a word, and went out to the phone booth near the pool. When he rejoined the breathless Bob-Whites, he was smiling.

"Pack up your troubles! You're as good as aboard!"

"The *Catfish Princess?*" Jim asked.

"I think so. Remember that retired riverboat captain, Captain Wainwarton, who talked at Sleepyside Junior-Senior High a while back?"

"*Do* I!" Jim answered. "He wrote a book about Mark Twain on the Mississippi. Jeepers, Dad, do you mean that you talked to him?"

"I did. I just remembered that he was from St. Louis. Guess what. He's part owner of the *Catfish Princess.* He remembered the Bob-Whites. At least, he said he remembered Trixie. Everybody remembers Trixie"—Mr. Wheeler smiled—"one way or another."

"A left-handed compliment if I ever heard one," Mart said. "Guaranteed not to swell your head, Trixie. Do you mean, sir, that we really will get to ride on the *Catfish Princess?*"

"I don't mean anything else, Mart. There's only one obstacle. The *Princess* will be bound for New Orleans. The journey there and back would take lots longer than the time we have."

"Then, why did you say we could pack?" Honey asked, deflated.

"I'm getting to that, Honey. Towboats stop at many intermediary points to unload freight, drop off empty barges, or pick up new loads. Captain Wainwarton suggested that you might want to ride the *Catfish Princess* to Cairo, Illinois, for instance. He said that such a trip would be very interesting."

"Hannibal, I'll bet a penny!" Mart's voice rose with excitement. "Oh, boy, have I ever wanted to see that Huck Finn country!"

"Sorry, Mart, but Hannibal is *up*river from St. Louis. We'd better be thankful for *any* ride and not be so particular about where we go."

"Maybe we can drive up there later," Mart said quickly. "It's one place I'd sure hate to miss."

"Anyplace on the Mississippi must be interesting," Trixie said, frowning at Mart.

Mr. Wheeler smiled. "Captain Wainwarton seemed to think so. He said something about a town where there are Indian mounds. He even mentioned a place along the river where Jesse James once hid."

"Say, I'd like to see that," Dan said enthusiastically. "It *is* Jesse James country, this Midwest. But,

Mr. Wheeler, you said the towboat was going on to New Orleans. How would we get back up the river from Cairo?"

"You won't." Mr. Wheeler smiled as he looked at the Bob-Whites' faces. "I don't mean that you'll stay in Cairo for the rest of your lives. I mean that you won't come back on the river. I'll have to send a car to Cairo to pick you up the next day. How about it? Do you think you can be ready to take off from the waterfront in St. Louis tomorrow morning?"

Mart answered for the group. "Just give us a chance!"

"It's too wonderful ever to believe," Trixie told Mr. Wheeler breathlessly. "And don't think we're not grateful to you for all the trouble you've taken."

"Forget it! You'll be out from under foot for a couple of days. Another thing—Trixie and Honey won't find anything on the towboat that they'll risk their lives investigating."

Trixie opened her purse, pulled the crumpled papers halfway out, then quickly shut them in again and smiled—a slow, mysterious smile. She caught Honey's glance and winked. *It's a good thing,* she thought, *that I didn't show those papers we found to Mr. Wheeler. They may not mean anything, but if he doesn't know about them, he won't worry.*

# Something in the Air • 4

EARLY THE NEXT MORNING, the little car, bursting with Bob-Whites, nosed its way into the parking lot near the Two-Way Barge Company's loading docks.

"Dad said to hunt out a spot in a far corner," Jim said. "We can swing around this way on our return from Cairo, and I'll pick up the car again. Boy, they really get moving early in the morning here, don't they? Did you ever see this much activity in the New York harbor?"

Below them the waterfront bustled with industry. Busy harbor boats snorted and puffed as they eased huge barges alongside the docks for loading.

Cranes lifted their long noses into the air as one
of them lowered lumber to a waiting carrier and another picked up lengths of steel pipe to unburden a
barge from upriver.

As far up the river as the Bob-Whites could see
and down to the bend below them, barges massed in
a spreading fleet. Some of them, loaded with grain,
their covers battened down for protection against
rain, waited to be towed to waiting Diesel-engined
towboats resting out in the river. Some of them,
empty, waited for cargo as officers hurried about the
docks checking and rechecking.

Jim pulled the two small bags from the car, handed
them to Mart and Dan, and locked the car doors.
"Guess we'd better find a place to report," he told
the other Bob-Whites. "Maybe we're supposed to go
up to the warehouse office. Now, what's eating you,
Trixie?" He looked at her curiously.

Trixie gestured mysteriously to a black car parked
in the opposite corner of the lot. "That Mercedes! If
you don't think Pierre Lontard even knows we're
alive, what's his car doing in this parking lot?"

Mart snorted and pointed to another Mercedes
nearby. "I suppose you think that one is his, too, and
that one over there near the building. Every black
Mercedes you see has to be that Frenchman's car,
Trixie."

"Only *his* car has the left rear hubcap missing," Trixie said triumphantly. "Honey noticed that right away. Anyone who even pretends to be a detective would notice a thing like that."

"You win!" Mart acknowledged. "But wouldn't he have even more business down around these parts than we do, if he's trying to buy an old steamboat? I guess you didn't think of that, did you?"

"No, I honestly did forget that," Trixie admitted. "I still think it's queer that Pierre Lontard turns up everyplace we go." She paused. "Is that someone from the office waving to us?"

A man wearing a captain's cap came toward the Bob-Whites, smiling. "I was told to keep an eye out for you. Good morning!" He shook hands with all of them. "I'm Captain Martin of the *Catfish Princess*. We're glad we're going to have you with us for a part of our tour. I wish you could go beyond Cairo. The lower river, from Natchez to New Orleans, is the most interesting part. We navigate the boat there by guess and by golly, mostly, for the river is shallow and shifty."

"We're ever so glad to have a chance to go on the river at all, Captain Martin," Honey said cordially. "Daddy suggested that we try to keep out of the way as much as we can."

"When you get to know Trixie, over there, you'll realize that statement doesn't mean a thing," Mart

said. "Honey and Trixie are girl detectives. If anyone
drops an anchor, Trix will scour the river bottom for
it."

"And come up with it, nine times out of ten," Jim
said loyally. "The Belden-Wheeler Detective Agency
is going to take a vacation for a couple of days . . .
or I think it is." He looked inquiringly at Trixie. She
smiled but said nothing.

Captain Martin seemed perplexed. He rubbed his
brown beard. Then he laughed heartily. "Oh, I see.
It's a joke, isn't it? Sometimes I wish we had detectives on board but not two young girl detectives.
This towboat is an island all to itself out in the
river. In fact, it will be well for you to keep your
stateroom doors locked when you're not there. Anything can happen. Something already did, this morning. Our cook didn't show up. I was really up against
it. Cooks are important. They rank as officers and get
the same pay, and there's plenty of reason for that.
Well, here we were, ready to leave, and no one to fix
the chow. We'd have had murder right and left,
Trixie, and lots of cases for a detective to handle if
the crew had to be put on limited rations."

"Jeepers! Maybe Honey and I could do the cooking. We could try. We can cook pretty well. . . ."

"I'm sure of that. Thanks for the offer. A crazy
thing happened, though. I'd just been informed that
our regular cook had to go to the hospital, when a

couple showed up. They're man and wife and wanted to sign on as cook and deckhand. The woman says she's had service on other boats. Of course, I haven't had time to check. Keep your fingers crossed. I know kids like good food, too."

"Heavens! We don't mind what we eat or where we sleep or anything else," Trixie said quickly. "We have to pinch ourselves to see if we're really here! It's surely good of you to let us go on the *Catfish Princess*. Is she one of those boats out there in the river?"

"Yes, sirree!" Captain Martin said proudly. "She's *the* boat, just coming in to pick up her fleet of barges ... the biggest one out there, a nine-thousand-tonner! She's one of two that the Two-Way Barge Company owns. They're the biggest boats in the country right now. Cost almost a million dollars apiece!"

Mart shaded his eyes to look. "Wow! Are we ever lucky! When does she sail, sir?"

"We'd hoped to get away around noon. This business of the new cook has slowed us up a little. We're towing grain—twenty barges. They're ready to take the first ten out now. See them lined up two abreast down there in the center of the wharf? Do you want to go out with them or wait for the rest of the tow?"

"Now!" the Bob-Whites chorused.

"All right. Do you think you can make it by yourselves?"

"Sure! As my sister told you, we don't want to be

in the way. Don't bother. We'll get aboard all right."
Jim herded the Bob-Whites together, and they
hurried down to the dock. A deckhand told them
where to board the lead barge and helped the girls
step over to its flat top. There they all stood, waving
to Captain Martin as a busy little harbor tug took the
clumsy load out to join the towboat.

On board the glistening white *Catfish Princess*, the
Bob-Whites were wide-eyed and curious. Passing the
galley, they saw the cook and maids busily opening
crates of vegetables, huge carcasses of meat being
swung into the mouth of a mammoth refrigerator,
and cases of canned goods and gallons of milk being
unpacked. Already the enticing smell of roasting
meat filled the galley, laced with the tang of baking
cherry pies.

"Up this way," a maid directed them. "Your cabins
are down this corridor. The girls are here, and this
four-bunk room is for the boys. Officers' quarters are
on either side of you. I hope the new cook and her
husband don't snore, for they're right next to you
girls."

Trixie stood at the door of the stateroom, amazed
at its snowy whiteness and comfort. "It's super! See,
Honey, isn't it perfectly perfect?"

"There's a lounge around the corner," the maid
continued, "and there are magazines there."

"Thanks again, but, jeepers, we want to go out on

deck and watch the river!" Trixie and Honey lifted their bag to the bunk. "We'll just get out of your way," Trixie told the maid.

The wide river stretched all around them. It swarmed with craft of every description—speedboats on their way to Alton Dam; rowboats; and puffing, protesting tugs. Across the river lay Illinois and busy East St. Louis. Ahead of them, as the tow assembled length after length of grain barges, the deckhands swarmed. They were checking and tying and carrying rope lines, wire, and steel chains.

The visitors watched, wide-eyed. "It's delirious!" Trixie called. "All this running around, all that loading machinery at the dock, all those deckhands out there swarming like ants. . . ."

"All the loads they carry—heavy ropes and chains! There's a kid out there no older than I toting a ton of chain. I saw him on shore before we came out here. His name is Paul. Look at him!" Mart leaned over the rail to watch a curly-haired, deeply tanned boy lower his load. He looked up, grinned, and waved his hand in salute.

"His uncle is a pilot. Paul wants to be a towboat pilot, too."

"It didn't take you long to get his life history. I didn't even see you talking to him," Trixie said.

"You were too busy stalking that Frenchman. Paul's been working on this boat for over a year. He

said he nearly died at first, because the work was so
hard. His uncle got his start as a roustabout on the
levee, then worked as a deckhand, and years later
got his license. That's what Paul wants most in all the
world. Come to think of it, I may want to be a river
pilot myself one of these days, instead of a farmer."
Mart sighed blissfully. "All this commotion! All this
excitement!"

"All that hard work!" Brian added. "You can hear
those men groan, even above the noise of the Diesel
engines. It takes muscle and sweat to clamp steel
cables to timberheads and lock the barges together.
Look at them turning those ratchets. Boy! They have
to chain them so close you can't get a dime in the
crevices."

"That's so they won't break loose. They leave a
cable they call a 'stern line' running from each side
of the after barges back to the boat," Mart said learn-
edly. "It holds the barges in line; it keeps them from
spreading out like a fan when they have to back up."

"Heavens, Mart, did you learn all that from Paul?"

"Partly. That kid knows everything there is to
know about the river, Trix. I asked some other men,
too, while we were waiting on the levee. The only
way you can find out anything is to ask."

"I thought Trixie was our official interviewer," Jim
said.

"I just pick other people's brains and take credit

for being smart," Trixie said. "I don't know what I'd ever do without any one of the Bob-Whites to help me out."

Mart put his hand on his hip and spun around with dancing steps.

> "Oh, I am the cook and the captain bold
>       An' the mate of the *Nancy* brig,
>    An' a bo'sun tight, and a midshipmite,
>       An' the crew of the captain's gig."

The other Bob-Whites joined Mart in a sailor's hornpipe. The maid rested her dust mop and stood openmouthed. Down below, on the gunwales, the hands, sweating and straining, heard the singing and looked up, grinning. The beat of the powerful twin-screw Diesel engines seemed to accent the rhythm.

"Cheese it!" Mart shouted suddenly. "Here comes Captain Martin. He'll think we've lost our marbles. The boat must be about to take off. Paul and the other hands down there are standing ready to hitch the tow to the front of the *Catfish Princess*. Golly, look at the acres of barges up ahead!"

The captain waved to the Bob-Whites, then went up a few steps into the pilothouse. There he talked with the pilot on duty and took his seat at the controls. Accurately, slowly, he eased the big boat till its snub nose touched the rear of the long chain of

barges, hardly jarring them. Then, as the nose of the
towboat closed against the barges, deckhands fastened tow and boat together with huge chains and
steel cables. The Bob-Whites watched, fascinated, as
the struggling, sweating men worked.

"Boy, it'd take an earthquake to jar that tow loose,"
Jim said, his eyes following every move the men
made.

"Yeah!" Brian agreed, awed. "Say, that guy down
there is signaling. It looks like we're ready to move!"

A whistle snarled. The big towboat shivered, as
though with relief. The engines accelerated, and the
gleaming *Catfish Princess* swung her tow into mid-
stream and headed south.

"It's heavenly! We're floating!" Trixie said blissfully. "Do you suppose we'll stay this close to shore all
the time?" She held Honey's hand and watched, eyes
wide and dancing. "I can even see a dog running
along that bank."

Two sharp blasts of the whistle sounded.

"I can see your lips moving, Trix," Mart shouted,
"but I can't hear a word you're saying. That's the
chow whistle. I'm starved. Let's get under cover.
Dibs on the first place at table!"

In the dining room, Captain Martin pointed out
seats the Bob-Whites should take, drew back Trixie's
chair, and motioned the maid to start serving.

"We can't stand on ceremony," he announced. "We only have half an hour to eat. We're past the first watch now . . . over an hour. I usually take over from twelve to six P.M., then from midnight to six A.M. again. Excuse me if I wade into my food. Take all the time you want. You've nothing to do but look at the river and eat. Right now, I have to hurry."

Food began to load the table—steaming mashed potatoes with rich brown gravy, roast beef, corn, peas, salad, applesauce, hot rolls, jelly, jam, catsup, pickles, milk, coffee, tea. Deep dishes fairly flew from hand to hand. Conversation stopped. Down below, the engines throbbed. A clatter of dishes and the sound of good-natured shouts came up from the crew's dining room.

The officers ate hurriedly, slid back their chairs, and disappeared. "Three kinds of pie coming," Captain Martin whispered to Trixie and Honey as he left.

When the officers had gone, a tired, red-faced woman slid into a place at the table. She was obviously the new cook. "It's good to sit down," she told Trixie. "I'm new here, and everything's hard to find in the kitchen."

"It's no wonder you're tired," Trixie said sympathetically. "All this perfectly perfect food!" She patted her full stomach. "Captain Martin said you just joined the *Catfish Princess* this morning—you and your husband."

"That's right. I'm Elena Aguilera, and my husband is Juan Aguilera. He's having a harder time of it today than I am, because he's out of condition. The work on deck is hard, and he's not used to it."

Trixie listened to the woman's words, which were spoken in a soft, cultivated voice. Her puzzled expression brought further explanation from Mrs. Aguilera. "We're glad, my husband and I, to have a chance to join the crew of the *Catfish Princess*. You see, he is writing a book about the great rivers of America, and I try to take pictures to add to his book. With almost no passenger boats on the river, this is the only way we can get material. I've always been a pretty good cook, and my husband knows much about all kinds of boats."

"You're a marvelous cook!" Brian, across the table, told her.

"How fascinating to be writing a book!" Trixie added.

"How can you take pictures when we're on the move?" Dan wondered. "Motion pictures wouldn't be any good for a book, would they?"

Mrs. Aguilera glanced at him quickly. "You're right. But I think we will tie up at shore from time to time between here and New Orleans. I think they will stop to let off barges and take on new ones. If it happens when I'm off duty, I'll get some pictures. What are you girls going to do after you finish your lunch? I've been all over the boat, and I know it pretty well. Would you like to go exploring with me?"

"We'd love it! That is, if it isn't too much trouble. But aren't you too tired?"

"No. This cup of tea was just what I needed. My quarters are just next to yours, I think. I'll see you there."

"Now, what do you think of that?" Trixie asked in a low voice as the girls went up to their cabin.

"What do I think of what?"

"That cook. What's an educated woman like her doing in a job where she has to work so hard?"

"She wanted to get on the river. You heard her say that. Just the same as we did. It's the only way she can get to see the country from the river. That's what she wants for her husband's book."

"I wonder what he's like," Trixie said thoughtfully. "I know what he *looks* like, of course, but who is he, really?"

"An author, I suppose, just as Mrs. Aguilera said."

Trixie didn't seem to hear Honey. "She said she was so tired, and now she's going all over the boat with us. It's just odd, that's all. I can't figure her out."

"Oh, Trixie! She wants to be kind to us. Maybe she has daughters of her own. Sometimes I think Mart may be right—that we're always imagining things."

"All right. You just wait and see. Something very

strange is going on around here."

"It's funny, but I have the same feeling, Trixie. Oh, not about Mrs. Aguilera. I like her. But there's something in the air, as sure's you're born."

# Moonlight Music • 5

Honey and Trixie, led by Mrs. Aguilera, climbed the few steps to the pilothouse. Captain Martin, seated in front of the levers, greeted the girls cordially. Then he looked inquiringly at Mrs. Aguilera.

"I'm showing the young ladies around, sir," she said. "They didn't seem to know where to go. The sandwiches are made, and dinner is under way...."

"It's so beautiful up here," Trixie sighed. The pilothouse windows were open. The boat drifted slowly, its engines little more than idling. They were hugging the shore so closely that they could hear birds chattering in the willows. From beyond the trees, a bobwhite whistled, clear and loud. Without thinking, Trixie answered the call with a shrill *bob-white!*

Captain Martin, startled, looked up quickly. Trixie covered her mouth and giggled. Honey laughed, too. Then Trixie explained. "You see, the name of our club at home in Sleepyside, New York, is the Bob-Whites, and the call of the bobwhite is our club whistle. We all belong to the club—Jim, Brian, Dan, Mart, Honey, and I. Oh, yes, and another girl, Diana Lynch. She couldn't come with us. The Bob-Whites always answer the call when we hear it, and that's what I did, without thinking."

"Interesting, I must say," Captain Martin remarked, evidently still a little confused. "Now, right ahead you can get a clear view of the river." He pointed way ahead, past the tow. "On your right you'll see Cahokia. It used to be inhabited by Indians —mound builders. If you'll look through these binoculars, you can see some of the mounds. Cahokia was the first settlement in Illinois; it is older than Chicago. The old paddle-wheeler *Shepherdess* struck a snag just about here, in 1844. Seventy people went down on her. In 1849, the *Bates* caught fire, then drifted toward shore and set a whole fleet of boats burning. Happened right over there." He shook his head at the thought.

Fascinated, the girls listened to river history and

legend, while Mrs. Aguilera made notes for her husband's book.

The captain showed how the boat controls worked. He even let Trixie move one of the levers and watch the tow respond to her slight touch.

"You'll find plenty to do, girls," he told them when they thanked him and started down the stairs. "Hunt around anywhere you want. Nothing can harm you. Just watch your step when you walk on the barges. Go way to the end if you want. The boys are halfway there now. They look like pygmies from here, don't they? If the cook doesn't have time to go with you, you can easily get around by yourselves."

"We don't want to take your time," Trixie told Mrs. Aguilera politely. "As Captain Martin said, we'll just hunt around by ourselves."

"Oh, I have plenty of time. I like to go over the boat and tow myself. I'll go with you, at least along the catwalks on the barges. It may be safer if I do."

"You don't know the places we've been . . ." Trixie began.

"Or the risks Trixie's taken!" Honey added quickly. "Jim—he's my brother—often calls her 'Intrepid Trixie.' "

"So, you see, we really can get along without—" Trixie interrupted sharply.

She stopped suddenly as Honey nudged her. Startled, Trixie continued. "Er . . . that is, we'll just

stop in our cabin and get our scarfs. The wind is
coming up." Trixie hurried off, with Honey close
behind her.

"Now, why did you have to act so impolite to her?"
Honey asked Trixie when Mrs. Aguilera was no
longer in sight. "She's probably lonesome and trying
to be kind."

"That's what you think. She's following us. That's
what she's doing."

"Trixie Belden, you have the most suspicious
mind!"

"Look who's talking! We *have* to be suspicious to
be good detectives. I told you before, and I'll tell you
again: Something strange is going on."

"If there is, I don't think she's involved in it,"
Honey declared firmly. "Say, what's that noise? It's
coming from the Aguileras' stateroom. She's not
there. She's waiting for us downstairs."

The girls stopped and stood quietly before the door
of the cabin next to their own. Just then a blast from
the whistle atop the pilothouse shrilled.

"Darn!" Trixie shouted into Honey's ear. "I can't
hear a thing now. What did you think you heard?"

"I don't know. There *is* someone in there."

"If it hadn't been for that old whistle we could
have been sure. . . . What did you say?"

"I said we're both pretty silly. Mr. Aguilera lives
in that stateroom, too. He's probably taking a nap."

"Of course. There's Mrs. Aguilera down there on deck. Hi!" The girls hurried over to meet her.

The three of them stepped down carefully from the deck of the *Catfish Princess* onto the nearest barge. There they saw Mr. Aguilera working over a rope. When he saw his wife and the girls, he waved, then bent over his work again.

"*Now* what do you think?" Trixie whispered as they stepped ahead of the cook. "If you did hear someone in that stateroom, it certainly wasn't Mr. Aguilera."

"Oh, I heard someone, all right. What that someone has to do with the mystery, and what the mystery *is*, I don't know. I've never been so puzzled. Look here, we're not being very polite, running way ahead of Mrs. Aguilera."

"We didn't mean to run so far ahead," Trixie called back to the cook. "I guess we were just excited." Aside to Honey, she whispered, "If she really is a cook professionally, then I'm a chimpanzee."

Honey made a gesture of impatience at Trixie's suspicion, then lagged to examine a marking on the side of the barge.

Mrs. Aguilera and Trixie walked on to the farthest barge. "How small and far away the towboat seems from here!" Trixie said. "It's miles!"

"Cool and quiet and still," Mrs. Aguilera said slowly, her eyes narrowing to tiny slits. "Far away from everything, from everyone."

Something in the tone of her voice and the expression on her face sent a wave of icy fear over Trixie. Before she could analyze the reason for her feeling, Mrs. Aguilera crowded her close to the edge of the barge. "Right over here, Trixie. There are *very* interesting things to see down below in the water. Bend your head. Closer! I'll hold your purse."

As the cook spoke, Trixie's feet shot out from under her and she plunged forward, screaming in fright. Frantically she clutched at the slack stern line and hung, struggling for a foothold, above the swirling current. "Honey! Honey! My purse!" Her frenzied call was drowned in the sound of water as it slapped against the barge side. In a split second, Honey was leaning over the edge, looking down at Trixie. "Hold tight!" she commanded. "Hold on to that rope, Trixie! Mrs. Aguilera! Mrs. Aguilera! Reach down for her! Save her!"

As though she were startled from a trance, the cook threw herself prone on the barge deck, seized Trixie's arms, and drew her up to safety. Shaking convulsively, Trixie looked around her, dazed. "What happened? Where's my purse . . . my purse?" Her voice trembled. She looked from Mrs. Aguilera to Honey, questioningly.

"Can't you see? Mrs. Aguilera has it!" Honey cried. "She caught it as you went over. She saved it for you.

She saved you, too, Trixie. Oh, she *did* save you!"

"Thanks!" Trixie told the cook shortly. She took the purse from Mrs. Aguilera and tucked it firmly under her arm. "We might both have gone into the river, my purse and I."

"Sit here a minute and rest," Honey told Trixie, her voice shaking. "I don't like to be this far away from everyone. Let's at least go back to where the boys are."

"Yes, let's go right now," Trixie said. "Thanks, Mrs. Aguilera. We mustn't keep you any longer."

With a brief smile, Mrs. Aguilera left them and walked quickly toward the towboat.

"Now you've offended her," Honey told Trixie. "She *did* save your life!"

"I wonder," Trixie said slowly. "For a while it seemed touch and go which was more important to her—my purse or my life." She hastily checked the contents of her purse to be sure the papers were still safely there.

Honey put her arm tightly around Trixie. "It was a frightfully narrow escape. Oh, Trixie, you're not quite like yourself . . . not quite fair to Mrs. Aguilera!"

"Maybe not," Trixie admitted. "Maybe not, but it's the way I feel!"

When they joined the boys and Honey told them what had happened, Trixie said nothing. She listened quietly to what they had to say and told them that

she would try to be more careful in the future. All the
while, though, and for a long time after, she didn't
forget the odd look on Mrs. Aguilera's face just before
the accident.

Once out of the city area, the river flowed through
pleasant country. Jefferson Barracks showed up
against the trees. Streets in scattered neighborhoods
seemed to walk right down to the river in a friendly
fashion. Boys and girls waved from the bottoms of
overgrown bypaths. From the river itself came enticing smells of wet sand, dry sand, blossoming
shrubs, dank marshes, and the sweet fragrance of
willows. Occasionally a long-legged heron fluttered
its wings, then stood watching the tow slide by.

Soon the channel narrowed, and limestone cliffs
rose in ever ascending heights from both banks.
Hawks, disturbed by the noise of the Diesel engines,
spread their broad wings and screamed.

"Paul told me there's a cave somewhere along here
that runs back several hundred feet underground,"
Mart told the Bob-Whites. "That may be it right back
in there. See that black hole? That may be the
entrance. Paul said Jesse James hid there once when
about twenty men were chasing him. He shot every
one of them. Yes, he did—Paul told me so—and then
he got away."

"Missouri's full of caves," Jim said, adding, "I sure

never will forget that sinkhole in Bob-White Cave in the Ozarks, that one Trixie fell into. Gosh, Trixie, you were almost a goner that time."

Trixie leaned back against a barrel hatch and sighed dreamily. "I was almost a goner till all of you showed up to save me. Bob-Whites *always* show up when one of our members is in danger. That's usually me. And you're usually the one who leads the rescuers, Jim."

"Well, for heaven's sake, try and keep out of trouble." Jim's face was serious. "I don't like that narrow escape you just had, Trixie, way up there in front of the tow."

"Forget it! Say, I can imagine just the way Tom Sawyer and Huck Finn felt when they were floating down this river on their raft. Tom said, 'The sky looks ever so deep,' and it does."

"Yeah, and when Tom said to Huck, 'That's a mighty lot of water out there,' do you remember what Huck answered? Remember that, Mart?"

"Uh-huh. He said, 'Yes, and you're only lookin' at the top of it!' Gosh, do you suppose we'll get to go to Hannibal before we go back to New York? I'd sure hate to have to tell the kids at school that we were as near as St. Louis and didn't go there. Boy, would I love to see Jackson's Island!"

"Yeah, and that fence Tom Sawyer whitewashed!" Dan said.

"Why can't you be satisfied with the place we are now?" Trixie asked, looking up at Mart. "You wanted a ride on the Mississippi River, and here you are."

"Sure, here we are, and it's swell. But who brought up Tom Sawyer and Huck Finn, Trixie?"

"I did. I hope we *can* go to Hannibal, but right now I'm almost perfectly happy."

An hour sped by, then another. The cliffs grew higher and higher, their long shadows reaching across the quick-changing channel. Once a towboat came close. Everyone—both crew members and officers—crowded to the rails to gossip. From their huddle halfway back on the tow, the Bob-Whites waved lazily and happily. They watched the other boat as it labored back of its long tow of coal barges, watched it till it disappeared from sight. The sun dropped lower in the cloudless sky. On shore, birds fluttered, seeking their nests in the rocky ledges. A cool wind came up out of the east, and a whistle's sharp blast announced that dinner was waiting.

Protesting that they couldn't possibly be hungry again, the Bob-Whites ate all the fried chicken in sight. "Do you know what?" Mart asked as they left the dining room. "Paul plays the guitar. He belongs to a trio down in New Orleans. They sing folk songs."

"Do you suppose he'll sing some for us?" Honey asked. "Maybe out there in front, on top of a barge in the moonlight?"

"Will he!" Mart cried happily. "We've got it all fixed up. We're going to have our own hootenanny. Let's get going as soon as you're ready. We'll wait for you girls here."

At the top of the stairs that led to their cabin, the girls ran into Mr. Aguilera. When he saw them, he hastily tried to throw out his arm to cover a tray of food he held. His face reddened as he tried to push past them.

"I do hope no one is sick," Trixie said quickly. "Is Mrs. Aguilera very tired? That dinner she cooked was so good. Did you have to take a tray to her?"

"She's all right. I'm in a hurry." Mr. Aguilera pushed rudely past them.

"Well, what do you think was biting him?" Trixie asked Honey. "It's no crime to carry a tray to someone."

"Maybe something just upset him. Trixie, did you leave this door unlocked?"

"I don't think so. Especially since Captain Martin warned us to be sure and lock it. Is it unlocked?"

"It is. No harm done, though, as far as I can see. As long as we have our purses with us everywhere we go, there isn't much we could lose."

"It doesn't seem possible that there could be a thief on board. You'd think anyone who ever got a job on a wonderful boat like the *Catfish Princess* would never take a chance on losing that job, wouldn't you?"

Trixie pulled a warm sweater out of the bag and
handed it to Honey.

"Yes, and I like every person that I've met on
board. Captain Martin *did* warn us, though. So lock
the door and hold on to your purse, Trixie. I have
mine."

At the foot of the stairs, they met Paul, two other
deckhands, and a young girl from the Ozarks named
Deena, who waited on tables. Jim, Dan, Mart, and
Brian were with them.

Searchlights from the pilothouse threw a clear
white beam along the tow as the young people went
far ahead, to the deck of a lead barge. There they
huddled in a semicircle while Paul tuned his guitar.

Moonlight had changed the water to liquid silver.
River lights, indicating each point and bend in the
river, twinkled like fireflies in the bottomland. From
time to time, small fish leaped out of the water in
groups, flashed white in the searchlight, and disappeared. Opaque tongues of low-moving fog drifted
about.

*It's wonderful out here,* Trixie thought. *The stars!
The mist! We could be in another country. I love to
watch Paul tuning up his guitar and to hear the beat
of the Diesel engines. Deena's pretty. She reminds
me of Linnie at Uncle Andrew's lodge in the Ozarks.
I should think she'd get lonesome out here, never
seeing other girls her own age. The other maids seem*

*a lot older than Deena and aren't as friendly.*

The whistle on a passing boat moaned mournfully. Trixie shivered. *Fog . . . mist . . . that whistle. . . . It's eerie,* she thought.

"Where's your mind been?" Jim whispered. "This is the second time I've asked you that, and you haven't answered. You've been miles away. Boy, can Paul coax harmony out of that guitar!" He paused. "You can't beat this, Trixie—miles from nowhere, drifting down the river in the moonlight!"

Trixie loved it, too, and her clear voice rose as Paul led the singing.

"I'm a wandering towboat man
  And far away from home.
  I fell in love with a pretty little girl,
  And now I no more roam.

"Through wind and rain and fog and snow
  And dangers that she'll never know,
  I'll walk the barges, tote the chains,
  And watch the shoreline creeping by,
  For I love my girl, my pretty little girl,
  And I'll love her till I die."

Paul tapped his guitar and changed the tempo. "It's a thousand times more fun to play when someone sings along. Do you know this one?" he said as he strummed a few bars.

"*Do* we?" Dan said enthusiastically. They all sang:

> "Down in the churchyard,
> All covered with snow,
> My true love's a-lying;
> Hang your head low.
>
> "Mourn for my true love,
> Under the snow.
> Mourn for my sweet love;
> Hang your head low."

When they had finished with the words, they hummed the chorus dreamily. Paul rested his guitar on his knees. "I haven't heard harmony like that in many a day. Don't you know any songs from your part of the country?"

"Sure," Mart answered. "If you think that one we just sang about the graveyard is mournful, you ought to hear some of the songs they sing back home in New York."

Dan laughed. "No one can beat the Dutch along the Hudson River for scaring up ghosts. You know—songs like 'Headless Horseman.'"

"For heaven's sake, let's not sing that one!" Trixie exclaimed. "It makes me feel creepy. How about the one about Rip van Winkle? All you need to do is to strike a few chords now and then, Paul. Let's sing, Bob-Whites."

"We'll sing you a song of the Catskills, oh,
A song of the mountain men . . . oh.

"Rip van Winkle, on a stormy night,
Left his cruel wife and went up the height
Of the Catskill range, where Hudson's men
Played ninepins merrily, but when
They gave him a draught, he drank so deep,
It sent him into a twenty-year sleep.

"We'll sing you a song of the Catskills, oh,
A song of the mountain men . . . oh.

"When Rip awakened he yawned and said,
'Twenty years?' then rubbed his head,
Took up his stick, called his dog,
Set off for town in the morning fog,
Singing:
'Now many a man's been twenty years wed,
And many a man's been twenty years dead.
I'll take the second, you take the first;
Of all man's troubles, a wife's the worst.'

"We've sung you a song of the Catskills, oh,
A song of a lucky man . . . oh."

As the Bob-Whites sang, they swayed back and forth and clapped in rhythm. Deena and the young deckhands clapped along with them.

At intervals, a white searchlight swung over the singers, silhouetting them against the sky, then released them to darkness again. Its wandering beams startled quiet night animals and birds on shore. Once Paul pointed out the round bright eyes of a swimming deer.

Finally the moon passed under a cloud. Damp fog crept closer. Breathless and a little weary, the young people stopped singing. Paul yawned and lifted the guitar cord from around his neck. "Let's call it a day. Going along with me? I'm clear tuckered out."

Wordlessly and a little reluctantly, the Bob-Whites followed, walking the long length of the tow back to the nose of the *Catfish Princess*.

"Thanks, Paul!" they shouted as the Louisiana boy, Deena, and the other deckhands went down to the crew's quarters.

"We'll walk you to your door," Jim told the girls. "Let me have the key, Trixie. I'll open it for you. . . . Say, it's already open!" He snapped on the light. "Hey, what's going on in here? Everything's a terrible mess. I know you girls never left it like this!"

# Stowaway • 6

BEWILDERED, TRIXIE and Honey stood at the door.
Everything in the room had been overturned. Bureau
drawers were upended, and bedclothing was torn
from the bunks. Their cries brought Mrs. Aguilera
running from next door. Lights clicked on to illumi-
nate the semidarkness of the corridor. Mr. Aguilera
joined his wife.

"A thief's been here!" Trixie cried. "Call Captain
Martin!"

As she spoke, the lights went out.

"Who did that?" Jim demanded. "Put the lights

back on again! Someone went by. Dan, was it you?"

"No, but somebody almost jumped over my head in the dark. I heard him hit the deck below. Get him!"

The boys jumped down the steps and ran across the deck, the girls close after them. "I heard a splash!" Trixie called and ran to the rail. "Right over there!" she told Captain Martin, who had hurried out from the lounge.

"You say someone has jumped overboard?" he shouted.

"Yes, sir! If you look right out there you can see his head bobbing!" Trixie peered into the dark water between ship and shore.

"I can see a dark spot. It isn't anyone's head. It's a buoy. There's deep water there."

The searchlight found the spot where Trixie was pointing.

"It *is* someone swimming," Trixie insisted. "That dark spot is moving. Can't you see it?"

"I guess Captain Martin knows a buoy when he sees one, Trixie," Mart said quickly. "He knows every inch of the channel. Whoever dumped things upside down in your room *has* to be still on board. Captain Martin will take care of it, if you leave it to him."

"Never mind, Trixie," Captain Martin said soothingly. "I'll probably need your help to get to the bottom of this. The maid will put your room to rights. When you've taken an inventory, let me know what is missing. I'll go into it completely tomorrow, before you leave the boat at Cairo. As though I didn't have enough trouble! A barge broke loose, and that's why we're running so close to shore. We have to pull in and tie it up. One more delay, and we won't get to Cairo till next week! Everyone out on deck!" he told the hands. "We've a lot of work to do!"

The Bob-Whites were up at the first tinge of dawn and ready for breakfast with Captain Martin. "I've checked with every member of the crew," he told them. "I can't find a clue to who might have gone through your things. Did you miss anything?"

"No, but. . . ."

"Yes, Trixie?"

"I honestly don't think that anyone who belongs on this boat upset our room. Someone *did* jump into the water and swim to shore. We know that for sure."

The Bob-Whites agreed vigorously. "That guy practically knocked me on the head making for the stairs," Dan said.

"It couldn't have been anyone on board," Captain Martin mused. "I know every single soul on board, and they're all here. Not since I've been captain of the *Catfish Princess* has there been a stowaway on board. Where could a man hide?"

"I don't know," Trixie answered. "But a man *did* hide somewhere."

Impressed with her earnestness, Captain Martin said quietly, "It *was* a buoy you pointed out to me in the water . . . that is, if we were looking at the same thing. I made every inquiry I could along the shore, over ship-to-shore phone, and again after we tied up to fasten that barge. No one saw anything of a swimmer. I'll admit there weren't many people around at that time of night. Just two men fishing and a couple more hanging around the levee. None of them had been in the water. It surely puzzles me."

Trixie looked around her to see if Mrs. Aguilera was within hearing distance. "Before we started singing, we met Mr. Aguilera carrying a tray out of their room, and I asked him if Mrs. Aguilera was tired and he had taken it to her, and—"

"Yes, I know, Trixie. Mrs. Aguilera thought you might remember that and mention it. She explained it to me. When she and her husband came aboard in the early morning to fill the emergency vacancy, they hadn't had their breakfast. They took some coffee and rolls into their cabin, and they hadn't had a chance to return the tray to the galley. So, you see, that clue's out. However, you keep up your detective work, Trixie. The Belden-Wheeler Agency may still come up with the answer. In the meantime, I'll turn in a report to the office in St. Louis. I've had thieves on board before, but they always stole something, and we tracked them down."

"Then you don't intend to try to find out who the stowaway was? You can make fun of Honey and me and our agency if you want to, but we've tracked down some pretty mysterious people—"

"I'm sure you have. In the first place, I don't honestly believe that there was a stowaway on board or that anyone jumped overboard. As I told you, the water back there is awfully deep, and no one who knows the river would ever try to swim it. Some pretty ugly fish live in the depths."

"How big?" Mart asked, instantly alert.

"Paddlefish up to two hundred pounds."

"Jeepers!" Trixie's blue eyes popped.

"You never thought the Mississippi had fish that big, did you, Trixie? Well, it does. A paddlefish looks something like a shark. Say, did you ever see a catfish ... a really big catfish?"

"How big?" Mart asked again.

"Six feet long. Very ugly ... blue black ... popeyes ... barbels that jut out."

Honey nudged closer to Trixie.

Captain Martin smiled. "You ought to hear the Cajuns down around New Orleans tell about big fish. If you were only going there with us, I'd have Shanty Jim, on the levee there, tell you about a garfish he saw. 'Old One-Eye' he calls him. Jim swears that he wears a gold crown and smokes a pipe, pushes up sandbars for tows to go aground on, and swishes his tail to make currents—and even that sometimes, when he gets hungry, he picks off a deckhand for lunch!"

Trixie and Honey, who had sat listening, relaxed and laughed.

"Laugh if you want to," Captain Martin said. "I long ago learned not to laugh at any legend I heard about the river. I'll tell you one thing: Roustabouts along the river give Old One-Eye a wide berth. When they get all tuckered out, they drop tobacco in the water for the old garfish. They like it when he lights up his pipe. The smoke gets thicker than fog, and boats have to tie up. Then they get a rest from totin' bales of cotton. See?"

"No, sir, I don't," Trixie said solemnly. "But to get back to that man who jumped overboard—"

"Forget that for the present, Trixie. I'm going on watch now. Come up to the pilothouse for a clear view of the river. It's a beautiful morning."

As the *Catfish Princess* faithfully prodded its long tow toward Cairo, Captain Martin, sensing the restlessness of his visitors, talked.

"The river's in my blood. It's been in my blood since I was a baby, for I was born in sight of the Mississippi. I was a lad of ten, running errands on the levee in St. Louis, when I made up my mind that life on the river was for me. Steamboats carried freight and passengers in those days. I got a job watching the roof of the pilothouse on the *Crazy Nell*, because sparks from the engine could set a boat afire. I was scared to death on my first job—scared I wouldn't make good.

"I was young. I didn't touch a hundred pounds on the scales. I tried to lift the chains and heavy ropes, but I couldn't make it. I couldn't even lift a bag of grain. I kept at it, though, and when I was fifteen, I was toting big loads and getting ten cents an hour. That wasn't much, but I had my keep on the boat. On shore, I could get dinner on the waterfront for twenty cents, and a movie cost a nickel. I could outfit myself in used clothes for a dollar, in a store on the wharf, and pick up a pair of shoes for a quarter."

"New shoes?" Mart wondered.

"Oh, no! Used shoes, but with a lot of wear still in 'em. Well, after that I worked as a deckhand, still on the *Crazy Nell*. Then I got to be steersman."

"Then you became a pilot?" Trixie asked.

"No. It took me three years before I got a pilot's license. By that time, I knew every inch of the river, every bend, every cliff, the ghost trunk of every sycamore—you ought to see one of them shine out in the searchlight on a foggy night. I could even shake hands with swamp frogs and call 'em by name. I was one pretty chesty kid when I got my first license. It was up to me, then, to steer my boat safely through the channel into Memphis port. I was a scared kid then, too. Now I've also got licenses on the Ohio, the

Missouri, the Tennessee, and every tributary that
flows into the near three-thousand-mile length of the
Mississippi—the Ouachita, Bayou Mason, Yazoo,
Sunflower. . . . When the Diesel engines came on, I
was whipped for a while. Now I'm all right, but I still
like the churn of the paddle wheels and the lonesome
call of a steamboat whistle on a winter night."

In their cabin, an hour or so before they were to
leave the boat at Cairo, Trixie told Honey, "Of course,
we know, both of us, that this business on board the
*Catfish Princess* ties in with Pierre Lontard."

"Sure it does," Honey agreed, "but how?"

"I'm not sure. He *was* on board. That I know, even
if Captain Martin doesn't think anyone jumped overboard. He *was* after my purse and those papers. How
he came to be on board, I don't know. Dan swears
someone jumped over him and ran across the deck.
There are only three staterooms in our corridor—ours
and the boys' and the Aguileras'."

"That's right. And that tray Mr. Aguilera was
carrying still sounds suspicious to me."

"Another thing, too, Honey. Why did Mrs. Aguilera seem so interested in my purse when I stumbled
out there on the barge?"

"Well, you can forget any idea you may have that
she made you stumble. Didn't she risk her own life
to pull you back? No, I think she's perfectly all right.

She's been so kind and friendly. Maybe her husband's a queer one, but I don't even have any reason to say that. Captain Martin never questioned their explanation of the tray."

"You must remember that Captain Martin doesn't know anything at all about the Lontard business. I was going to tell him, till I remembered how much fun he made of our detective agency."

"He didn't mean anything by that. Most grown-ups don't take us seriously till they know of the good work we've done—you, especially."

"Maybe so. Something else bothers me. I *wish* Mrs. Aguilera hadn't heard me give the Bob-White whistle."

"Well, it really is supposed to be a secret. If that bobwhite hadn't whistled from a nearby field on shore . . ." Honey mused.

"I know. And when I heard it, I just answered, without thinking. After I'd done it, I felt sort of silly and thought I had to say something. I wish I weren't so gabby."

"You're not," Honey said warmly. "You're just friendly. Everybody loves you for it. As for worrying about Mrs. Aguilera—I wish you wouldn't. I think I know people pretty well, and I'd trust her with anything. She's so motherly. Now the boys are calling us. Hear them?"

"Yes. We must be getting pretty close to Cairo.

And, Honey, you may think Mrs. Aguilera is motherly
and all that, but she's not one bit like my mom. Say, I
kind of hate to get to the end of our trip, don't you?"

"Kind of," Honey said slowly.

Trixie opened the bag, shoved her pajamas and
slippers inside, and added a kit with her brush, comb,
and lipstick. "I know just what you mean. When
Pierre Lontard jumped overboard—and I'd stake my
life that's who it was—then our work on board this
towboat seemed to be finished."

She stopped packing, looked intently at Honey,
and continued, "This may be the biggest case we've
ever worked on—*if* we can prove those papers in my
purse have something to do with the space program,
and *if* we can follow up that Pierre Lontard. Jeepers,
Honey, think what it will mean to our agency. Do you
have anything to put in this bag?"

"A few things." Honey paused a moment. "Aren't
the engines slowing down?"

"Yes. We must be at Cairo."

"Then we must hurry. Captain Martin said he'd
have a harbor boat come out to take us to shore.
They aren't going up to the wharf with the *Princess*.
All the barges in this tow are headed for New
Orleans."

Trixie helped Honey add her possessions to the
bag. She checked her purse to make sure the papers
were safe. "It doesn't seem as though we've been

here more than a few hours, and think of the things that have happened! I love the *Catfish Princess*. I can't hear the engines at all now. Let's find the boys."

Politely and cordially, the Bob-Whites said good-bye to Captain Martin and all the other officers and crew members who had been so gracious to them on their cruise.

"You all come and visit us again. Now, see that you do!" Captain Martin told them. "When you get off the tug, go through Fort Defiance State Park to the motel, where you're supposed to meet the car. You can't miss the motel. It's right on the main street. Good-bye, now."

Mr. and Mrs. Aguilera stood watching, and Paul and Deena waved wistfully from the boat's rail as the water widened between the *Catfish Princess* and the chugging tug.

# Bob-White Luck • 7

I WONDER WHICH way we're supposed to go now," Jim said when the group reached the river's edge. He picked up one of the bags and motioned for Brian to take the other one.

"Straight through that park." Mart pointed confidently. "I'm sure the Heartland Motel is not far from the edge of it; just a few blocks, maybe."

"Then we won't need a taxi." Trixie took the scarf from around her sandy curls and stuffed it in her sweater pocket. "It's hot here, isn't it? It was so cool on the river. I hated to leave the *Catfish Princess*."

"Me, too," Honey said. "We didn't have time to know Deena at all."

"Or Paul," Mart added. "Do you want Dan and me to carry the bags now?"

Brian shook his head. Jim said, "No, thanks," and he swung the small suitcase he was carrying into his other hand.

After a few minutes of walking in silence, Jim called out, "We're practically there now. See the sign up ahead? I wonder why they call the motel 'Heartland.'"

"Because it's in the Middle West . . . heart of the land," Mart said pompously.

Dan sighed. "I wish the time would come when you wouldn't know all the answers, Mart."

"Can I help it if I'm just naturally bright? What's bothering you, Dan? Your face is as long as a sad alligator's."

"It's nothing. It's just that I can't help wondering about that sneaky Lontard. I wonder if it really was Lontard who stowed away. I wonder where he's going to turn up next."

"Captain Martin didn't think there was a stowaway on board," Mart said bluntly.

Dan rubbed his head ruefully. "He would have if someone had practically knocked his block off making for the rail."

"Maybe he drowned," Mart suggested cheerfully.

Trixie shuddered. "Oh, I hope not. Mart, you're bloodthirsty. I've been thinking about the same thing as Dan has, though. Of course Pierre Lontard swam to shore, and we haven't seen the last of him. Since we couldn't go all the way to New Orleans, I'll be glad when we get back to St. Louis. Even if Captain Martin didn't think a man jumped overboard, *I* know it was a man Honey and I saw swimming. It wasn't any buoy. That man was Pierre Lontard, too. He'll show up again. You just watch and see if he doesn't."

"I hope *I* watch and see the car we're to meet here," Brian said as he put down the suitcase he was carrying and brushed the perspiration from his forehead. "Do you think we should go inside the motel?"

"Of course," Jim answered. "Whoever's going to meet us wouldn't be waiting around for us at the door. They'd be inside someplace. Here, Dan, you take this bag now, and I'll go and look." Jim held the door open for the girls.

"We'll wait over here in the lobby for you," Trixie told him. "I hope we can get started back right away."

The Bob-Whites found seats facing the street.

"That park we walked through was pretty," Trixie said. "Some of the places we passed, though, looked pretty dilapidated. I guess that's because there aren't any steamboats anymore, and the town has probably moved away from the river. It's kind of sad, isn't it, Honey, for that to have happened?"

"Yes. It would be wonderful to have seen Cairo when steamboats were all over the two rivers, the Ohio and the Mississippi. Don't you remember the glamorous movie of Edna Ferber's *Showboat?* I used to think it would be neat to be born on the *Cotton Blossom,* as Magnolia Hawks was."

"And get to meet all those show people! I used to think Gaylord Ravenal was dreamy." Honey sighed blissfully.

"Gosh! Girls!" Mart threw one leg over an arm of the lounge chair, where he was sprawled. "Give actors some black, flashing eyes and shirts with ruffles on 'em, and girls don't care what's inside of 'em."

"That's not right, Mart Belden, and you know it," Honey said indignantly. "Men *were* handsome in those days, and you'll have to admit it."

"Why do you suppose the places around here have Egyptian names?" Brian changed the subject calmly. He couldn't stand it when the Bob-Whites argued. "We passed Thebes on the way down, and that's where Captain Hawks of your *Cotton Blossom* lived, Honey. Now we're in Cairo, only they call it 'Kayroh' instead of 'Kyeroh.' How come all this Egyptian stuff around here?"

"Well, you see, it was this way—"

"Not again, Mart! You don't know the answer again!" Dan hid his face in his hands.

"I do. When I wonder about anything, I try to find

the answer. Sometimes you just keep wondering. They call this area 'Egypt' because of all the rich delta land around here—like the delta of the Nile River. And it's because of all the corn, too, that they raise in this rich soil."

"Okay, Mart. That figures. Thanks. Just to keep the record straight, though, I don't spend all my time wondering."

"Dan sure doesn't!" Trixie said emphatically. "If you'd just give someone else credit once in a while, Mart, you'd realize you don't come up with *all* the answers. If Dan hadn't done anything but *wonder* about those jewel thieves in New York, I'd have been found somewhere with my throat slit."

"What the heck are you talking about, Trixie?" Jim had joined the group and stood listening. "You all sound as though you've been racketing about something. I'll give you something to bother about. The clerk at the desk said that no one has asked for any of us. He's sort of a wise guy. . . ."

"In what way?" Trixie asked.

"There are a lot of people around that desk. See them? I guess he was nervous. I asked him if anyone had inquired about someone named Wheeler. He said, 'I don't think so. I don't remember. People ask me a dozen questions a minute. Now, if you'd asked about someone called Schimmelpennick—I'd remember a name like that.' Of course, everybody laughed."

"That made him think he was a big shot, I guess," Mart said. "Did you tell him off?"

"In a way, I guess I did. I told him I thought Schimmelpennick was an honorable name, but I was inquiring about Wheeler."

"Thereby making an enemy of him," Mart declared. "Deflate a windbag, and you have. . . . What did you say, Brian?"

"I said it's obvious that the guy who was supposed to pick us up hasn't arrived," Brian said calmly. "It won't hurt us to wait here for a while. I like to watch traffic out there in the street. First thing you know, the car will drive up and park right in front of our eyes."

It didn't, though. No car drove up. No one inquired at the desk for anyone named Wheeler.

After the Bob-Whites had waited for two hours, Jim decided on action. "I'll go and place a call for Dad. We must have misunderstood him, or whoever was supposed to come after us must have had trouble on the way."

"We'll all go over to the booth with you," Mart said. "You have to place the call through that girl at the switchboard."

The Bob-Whites waited in a semicircle while Jim talked to the girl with headphones. They saw him hesitate, turn around to leave, then go back to talk to her again.

"Say, what do you know?" he told the waiting group. "Come over here by the window so no one can hear. There's skulduggery going on, for sure."

"Oh, Jim, what is it?" Trixie begged in a worried voice. "Is it something that Lontard man has done?"

"Looks like it, Trixie. It looks very much like it. When I asked the operator to put through the call to Dad in St. Louis, she told me it was the second call she'd put through to that number in the past few hours. She said a man telephoned Dad when she first came on duty at seven o'clock this morning."

Trixie put her hand to her mouth in dismay. "Did you find out what he told your father?"

"Not at first. I quizzed her about it, and she got sort of huffy . . . said she never listens in. I told her I was positive she never did intentionally. When I went on to explain why it was so important to us, she opened up a little."

"What did she say?"

"Just this, Trix: She heard the man tell Dad that we had decided not to stop at Cairo but to stay on the *Catfish Princess* and go on to Memphis instead; that the captain of our boat had talked to shore on the radiophone and said that we wanted this man to call Dad collect and tell him of our change in plans."

Trixie shook her head in bewilderment. "Now, why would he do a thing like that?"

"To give him a chance to snatch your purse," Dan

said positively. "When that cops-and-robbers act he worked up on the towboat failed, he must have thought up another one."

"Heavens! These papers must really be important to him!" Trixie opened her purse, slid the sheets out, examined and rearranged them, then closed the snap and tightened her hold. "I'm certain they're plans —figures concerning the space program. Somebody must be willing to pay a lot of money for the information we've got."

In her excitement, Trixie had raised her voice. Honey, aware of the fact that the desk clerk had left his post and passed very near them, held her finger to her lips to warn her friend.

"Yes, you'd better pipe down," Dan warned. "I'm beginning to think you're in over your head, Trixie. That Lontard looks to me like a bad one. He probably has his eye on us at this very minute."

Jim whirled around toward the motel desk. "If that's so, Dan, and I guess you're probably right, then we'd better get out of here. I'm going to jam that call through to Dad in a hurry, tell him what's happened, and see what he wants us to do. He may already have started a car on a wild-goose chase to Memphis." He hurried off to the telephone.

"Oh, I do hope Jim gets hold of Daddy right away," Honey said in a subdued, troubled voice. "We really don't know which way to turn, do we?"

When Jim returned, the Bob-Whites became even more worried. "I couldn't reach Dad," Jim informed them. "He went someplace with Mr. Brandio, and no one seems to know when they'll be back or how to reach them."

"That's just swell, isn't it?" Mart said. "Where do we go from here?"

"We try to find some other way of getting back to St. Louis—and in a hurry," Brian said.

"What will we use for money?" Mart asked realistically.

"Everybody empty out his pockets and see how much we have altogether," Jim ordered.

When the small bills and silver were counted, the amount came to thirty dollars and a few cents.

"I don't know why we don't carry more money with us," Honey wailed. "That won't be enough to pay all our fares on the train or bus."

"We don't carry more money because we never need it in Sleepyside," Jim reminded her. "Everybody knows us there. When we need anything, we can charge it."

"This isn't Sleepyside. We're hundreds and hundreds of miles from there. We're way down here in an old river town, and that Frenchman is just waiting to murder us!" Honey cried. "Jim, why don't you call Mr. Brandio's office and have them wire us some more money?"

"I don't want to do that, except as a last resort, Honey. I think Dad would be embarrassed. We're a fine outfit if we can't figure some way out of this. Do you suppose we could hire someone to take us back to St. Louis and have them collect the fare there?"

"Of course!" Honey cried triumphantly. "Jim, you find a driver for us!"

It wasn't as easy as it sounded, however. Not a taxi driver with whom they talked would make a run of such length. A crowd collected around the Bob-Whites. It was a sympathetic crowd, but no one was very helpful.

When they had been turned down the third time, a young man wearing a yachting cap arrived at the desk. "Are you kids in some kind of jam?" he asked.

"That's the name for it," Jim told him. "It's this way. . . ."

After Jim told the story, Mart, who had been fidgeting around impatiently, asked, "Any suggestions, buddy, on how to get back to St. Louis?"

The young man smiled. "This one. I've got an outboard cruiser I'm taking up to Alton Dam for a competition run to be held there tomorrow. If you want to crowd in, I'll take you along."

"Wow!" Mart shouted. "More of the old Bob-White luck! Let's go."

"We can pay you thirty dollars," Jim said practically. "If that isn't enough we can get more when we get to St. Louis and call my father."

"Why should I charge you, when I'm going there anyway?" the young man said with a smile. "I'll be glad to have some company."

"We couldn't let you go to all that trouble for nothing," Jim insisted. "Let us pay you what we have."

"Not a chance. Is this all of your gang?"

"I'm Trixie Belden," Trixie told him, holding out her hand. "We're grateful to you for a chance to go back to St. Louis right away. We'll find some way of showing you our thanks later. These are my brothers Brian and Mart. This is Dan Mangan, and Honey Wheeler and her brother, Jim."

"Call me Bob," the young man said. He didn't give his last name. "I'm ready to take off if you are. My car is out front. We can all get into it, if you don't mind crowding. The boat's over on the Ohio side. It's where all small craft dock. I'll leave my car on the levee there till I get back."

Trixie glanced at her watch. "Is there enough time for us to get some lunch? We had breakfast real early. I'm hungry. We can go into the coffee shop. It won't take long. Will you be our guest, Bob?"

"If you can make it snappy. I want to get going."

So they hurried through hamburgers, downed malted milks, bought several small packages of cookies to eat later on, and, when the sun was directly overhead, followed Bob to his car.

The run across Cairo took no time at all. Almost before they knew it, Bob pulled up and parked near a maze of masts and bobbing motorboats. He helped the girls into a shining varnished motorboat, the *Comet*.

"Man, this is a honey," Jim said, whistling. "You don't think we'll overload her, do you?"

"No, I don't," Bob said brusquely. "Just get in."

"This sure beats going to St. Louis by car," Mart said jubilantly. "We'll see what it feels like to zoom along the river, instead of the pace we went at on the *Catfish Princess*. Not that I didn't think that was super, too," he added quickly. "Need any help, Bob?"

"No, thanks." Bob cast off, got under way down the Ohio, around the bend of the huge lake formed by the confluence of the two rivers, and headed the *Comet* up the Mississippi.

"I guess we gave old Pierre Lontard the slip this time," Trixie whispered to Honey. "He thought he had us all nicely sewed up in Cairo. That for you!" She waved airily in the direction of the delta city, fast fading into the distance behind the motorboat.

Far from her sight, back in Cairo, a man walked hastily along the levee near the marina, climbed into his car, and hurriedly stepped on the accelerator of a black Mercedes.

# Rescued · 8

THE SPEED of the boat brought coolness with it. Trixie and Honey, their hair ruffled by the breeze, bent with the sway of the boat and laughed happily. They passed a towboat, its engines laboring as it pushed a heavy tow of oil barges upstream against the current.

"The *Catfish Princess* had it easy, just rolling along downriver, didn't it?" Mart asked. "Slow as it was, it makes me lonesome for it when I see another towboat. Boy, this one sure churns up the waves, doesn't it, Bob?"

Bob, his head bent over the wheel, didn't answer. He kicked angrily at the floor under him.

"I know what you're thinking, fella," Jim said. He had a speedboat of his own on the Hudson. "Those waves sure mess up the current, don't they?"

Bob didn't answer. He just kept his gaze fixed on the buoys that marked the channel line.

Thebes loomed up. Children stood on the hilltop on shore. The Bob-Whites waved to them. Bob slowed his boat, reached for binoculars under the seat and, holding them with one hand, looked intently past the shoreline toward the village.

A road paralleled the river. Cars and trucks sped along it. Bob's binoculars followed one car. Trixie, curious, could see very little without distance glasses. One thing seemed peculiar to her, though. It looked as if the car had its headlights on, or the sun's reflection gave that impression.

"What do you see, Bob?" she asked. "May I look?"

Bob turned quickly, shoved the binoculars under the seat, and stepped on the accelerator.

"It wasn't anything," he said shortly.

*I guess he forgot I asked him if I could use the glasses,* Trixie thought. *He's kind of edgy. I thought he'd be more fun. When we're out in Jim's boat at home, he's not a bit like Bob. Maybe the Mississippi River is different. It has such a strong current, Bob has to watch it every minute.*

Jim and Brian seemed puzzled, too, at Bob's odd behavior.

"Everyone around here is too sober," Trixie burst out. "Let's sing something." With a clear voice she led a song Paul had sung back on the *Catfish Princess*.

"Oh, the riverman's life is the life for me,
Hi diddle diddle de dee!
Out on the water yet near to the land,
Hi diddle diddle de dee!
Oh, I don't like the ocean with all of its
motion,
Hi diddle diddle de dee!
And I don't like the whales, or sea ser-
pents with scales,
Hi diddle diddle de dee!"

The putt-putt of the motor seemed to mark time as the boat sped on. Its driver paid no attention to the singing, however. He riveted his gaze on the shoreline.

As the Bob-Whites began to swing into the second verse, Bob straightened in his seat, took out his glasses again, and stared at the shore. He flashed on the boat's lights. "Just trying them out," he said to Jim, who was close enough to follow his movements. Suddenly the boat swayed. The engine sputtered, coughed, and stopped. They were running quite close to the shore, a shore that was swampy and completely deserted.

Bob pumped the accelerator and fooled with the controls.

"Anything I can do?" Jim asked helpfully. "I have a boat something like the *Comet*. Maybe there's water in the gas." He leaned down, put a little gas in his hand, and blew on it to see if some water remained after evaporation of the gas. "Nope, that isn't it."

"Just leave it to me. I'll get her going," Bob said curtly. He stepped on the accelerator again. The engine responded.

"Boy, that's a souped-up baby!" Jim said admiringly. "Bet she'll do fifty."

Bob made a gesture of impatience. "Just keep your hands off, buddy. I'm going to run her in here and see what's the matter."

He took his hand from the throttle, tipped the engine up from the water, and ran through a reed-filled swamp into a cove concealed by a maze of low-hanging willows. Just as the bow entered the cove, two men waded up to the boat. They were red-faced and angry.

"What in Sam Hill are you doin' in here?" one of them growled. "We've been spottin' a school of fish here for days. Just about to sink our lines. Now you've messed everything up. What's wrong with your boat?"

"Not a thing," Bob answered coldly, his eyes going past the men to the road on shore. "I just wanted a chance to look over my motor. It's been missing."

"Look her over then," one of the men said. "You can't do any more harm here. Well, ain't you gettin' out?"

Up on shore, a car's engine raced. Its wheels spun in the sand; then it roared up the road.

"I guess not," Bob answered, and he started the engine. "She seems to be working all right now." The boat purred perfectly as he backed out and swung it into the channel. "I guess I was mistaken," he called back to the angry men. "Better fishing next time!"

"Don't you think that was queer?" Trixie whispered to Honey as the boat sped on its course. "Bob's been acting sort of odd ever since we started, not a bit good-natured the way he was when he invited us on board. I wonder. . . ." She bent her head close to Dan. "Did you hear that car up on the road when we stopped? Bob seemed to be listening for it. Or am I crazy?"

"You're not crazy," Dan assured her. "Just pipe down. Keep quiet. Don't say a thing."

"Then you think something's odd, too?"

"I'm sure of it. Hush!"

Bob bent low over the wheel again.

The willowed shoreline whizzed by in a green blur.

Faster they went, and faster, throwing the spray high and white. The *Comet* fairly jumped through the water. The flying landscape changed from flat marshy land to sandstone cliffs that rose high above the shore. Jim's face turned white as they watched Bob steer into the track of a sailboat manned by two young boys. "Watch it!" he called sharply.

Bob only growled and sped ahead, breaking every river traffic rule.

Men in small boats shook their fists angrily as they rocked dangerously in the wake of the *Comet*. Towboats whistled sharp warnings as Bob ran perilously close to their crawling barges.

Trixie was certain now that there was something alarming about Bob's actions. There wasn't much to connect him with Pierre Lontard, yet she was sure he was in cahoots with the young man in some way. Could they have arranged a rendezvous at the spot where Bob ran into the fishermen? Bob had been furious when he saw the men.

Jim and Brian, sober-faced, relayed knowing glances to Mart and Dan, immediately back of them, and to the girls. They said little to one another, and what they did say was sometimes lost because of the roar of the boat's motor.

Trixie's mind went frantically back to the lobby of the Heartland Motel, where they had waited. She tried to remember anything that had happened there that might throw some light on Bob's behavior. When had she first noticed him? Not till they were dickering with the taxi drivers. No . . . that wasn't quite true. She had noticed a yachting cap on the head of someone in the lobby. Could Bob possibly have been Lontard's stool pigeon all the time? Could Lontard have stationed him at the motel to watch for the Bob-Whites? Had he watched for a chance to get them on his boat? Sadly Trixie thought: *We did something Moms has been warning us against ever since we could talk: We accepted a ride with a stranger.*

Trixie put her head close to Dan's. "I think we've been led into a trap," she whispered hoarsely.

Dan nodded. So did Mart. They knew, too.

In front of Dan and Mart, Jim turned around, bent his head meaningfully toward Bob's head in front of him, and held his finger to his lips.

What could they do? Very little. Recklessly as he drove, Bob wasn't going to do anything that would harm himself. So wrecking the *Comet* was out.

*Something, someone will be waiting to seize us, whenever and wherever he lands us,* Trixie thought. *That's it. That's why Bob was signaling, turning his lights on and off way back there when we were singing, just before he headed into that swamp. If the fishermen hadn't been there. . . .* Trixie shivered. Honey put her hand out and grasped Trixie's, and

Trixie squeezed hard. "Don't be afraid," she said as loudly as she dared. "Bob's just showing off how fast the *Comet* will go. Remember? He's going to race her tomorrow."

"I . . . don't . . . think . . . that's . . . it," Honey answered.

The *Comet* passed Cape Girardeau. It passed the levee of St. Genevieve.

*If Bob does happen to be in cahoots with Pierre Lontard, we'll know it when we get to St. Louis,* Trixie thought. *That's when we'll find out what he's up to.*

The *Comet* slowed as they approached Jefferson Barracks, far below the city. *This is it,* Trixie thought quickly. *Lontard will be waiting on shore for us. He's been following the road above the riverbank. Should we go overboard when he slows down? Would we be able to swim to some boat here in the river?* The faces of the other Bob-Whites were just as serious as Trixie's. Their eyes seemed to be seeking some avenue of escape.

Bob, intent on making shore, steered directly toward a grove of willows. Trixie moved closer to Honey, motioned to the other Bob-Whites to huddle, then said aloud, "Shall we swim?"

Bob, startled, turned around and snarled, "Try it! I have a gun for emergencies, and don't think I won't use it."

Trixie, horrified, looked out to the broad river. It was strangely, suddenly, bare of any water traffic. No boats? Far in the background, she saw white water churning, white water that quickly revealed two Coast Guard patrol boats bearing down on them. Smiles broke out on the faces of the Bob-Whites as Trixie pointed out the boats rapidly closing in.

Bob had taken his hand from the throttle to turn into a shaded cove. Then, alerted by the sudden silence of the Bob-Whites, he looked around. What he saw galvanized him into furious action. Snarling like a wildcat, he backed up, spun the *Comet* around, and headed for open water. His runabout, geared for speed, responded immediately. Quick as he was, though, he couldn't overcome the moments he had lost in reversing. The V of the approaching boats narrowed, plunging Bob's boat into the only channel he could follow—the one that led toward the nearest city dock.

"Don't try any funny business!" one of the Coast Guard seamen shouted. "Put in ahead, where you see that warehouse!"

Bob, one hand on the throttle, tried to reach below him, where the barrel of a rifle glinted in the afternoon sun. Trixie, seeing his gesture, shouted out, "He has a gun. He'll use it!"

The guardsman in the boat nearest the *Comet* drew his gun, leveled it at Bob's cold, white face, and said,

"One move toward that gun, buddy, and you'll never handle another one. Keep going!"

Like most other cornered culprits, Bob's resistance collapsed. He sagged like a balloon with the air released, kept his hand on the lever, and steered the *Comet* obediently into the dock. At the guardsman's command, Jim and Brian threw a line around the timberhead and made the cruiser fast. The guardsmen then commandeered Bob's rifle.

"All right, give me a ticket!" Bob said sullenly. "I suppose that's what you have in mind."

"It *was* what we had in mind when we first spotted you back there on the river," the officer said. "A ticket on almost all the counts you could have against you, beginning with no registration number on your boat and ending with reckless steering and endangering lives. It's a little more now, my friend. You did a good job of resisting back there, so we'll just go and talk it over at headquarters. Come along, now."

The Bob-Whites watched Bob, cursing under his breath, being led off. They were obviously relieved to see him go.

"Now we'll see what you kids have to say," one of the seamen said. "How are you hooked up with him?" He nodded toward Bob's back.

A small group of wharf hangers-on had collected, watching. Before any Bob-White could reply, two men stepped out of the crowd. One of them flashed a badge, spoke quietly to the Coast Guard men, and said in a loud voice, "We'll take over now. We have some questions to ask."

The seamen saluted and left.

"Now, who'll speak for the group?" one of the men asked.

Jim started to answer, but Trixie put her hand out to protest. "I think it depends on who is asking the questions."

"Secret Service, Trix," Dan said quickly. "What do you suppose they want?"

"We haven't done anything," Trixie said quickly. The other Bob-Whites echoed, "Not a thing!"

"We were stranded in Cairo," Trixie began, "and Bob—he's the owner of the *Comet*—offered us a ride back to St. Louis. You see, we live in New York. . . ."

"That's enough for now. We'll find out all the details later. I'd like to see your purse, young lady. May I please have it?"

Trixie looked wildly at Dan. "Do you *know* they're from the Secret Service? Are you sure it isn't another of Lontard's tricks?"

The man who asked to see her purse took his identification from his pocket and opened the folder to show it to the Bob-Whites.

Silently Trixie handed over her purse. The man

took the papers from it, quickly glanced at them, then nodded to the other man. "I guess you'll all have something to talk about at headquarters. You will please come with us."

It was a sadly dejected group that waited numbly for Mr. Wheeler and Mr. Brandio to appear at the federal building, where they were being held.

Only after long and detailed questioning by federal agents had they been allowed to telephone. When Mr. Wheeler heard Jim's voice, Jim reported, he was frantic. The driver of the car, sent on from Cairo to Memphis, had failed to make contact. Mr. Wheeler had telephoned authorities in Cairo, who told him of the Bob-Whites' departure by water. No one could tell him a thing about the boat they had used or the man who owned it. Mr. Brandio, summoned by Mr. Wheeler, had been trying to reach federal authorities for word of the young people when Jim's call came through.

"I've never known my dad to be so upset over anything," Jim said. "I guess we're really in trouble because we didn't tell him anything about this business before now."

Trixie's face fell. "I wouldn't have caused him any worry for the whole world," she said. "I *was* going to tell him everything just as soon as we saw him. I didn't have any idea we'd be held here. I was just so glad to get off the *Comet* that I didn't think of anything else. Honey, you know I wouldn't have worried your father if it could have been helped, don't you?"

"We all know that," Honey said, turning indignantly to Jim. "If you'll remember back a little way, Jim, you'll quickly realize that everything significant that has happened to us has happened *since* we embarked on the *Catfish Princess*. You'll remember, too, that we tried to get hold of Dad on the telephone at Cairo, and we found out someone—Lontard, we're certain—said we were going on to Memphis. I can't see where Trixie is to blame. In fact, I don't see any good reason why we have to be held here for questioning."

"It's routine," Dan told her. "The whole thing will clear up as soon as Mr. Wheeler and Mr. Brandio get here. What I can't understand is how the Secret Service men knew you had the papers in your purse."

"I can," Mart said quickly. "At least, I have an idea. That sneaky clerk at the motel in Cairo was hanging around listening to us talk, and he was looking right over Trixie's shoulder when she took the papers out of her purse back there in the lobby. Don't you remember, Trix, that Honey and Dan warned you to keep your voice down and close your purse?"

"I do remember now," Trixie replied. "I suppose the clerk thought we were all working together— Lontard, Bob, and all of us Bob-Whites. Heavens!

Maybe the Secret Service doesn't even know that Bob is mixed up with Lontard . . . or that we think he is. Oh, dear, maybe they don't even know anything about Lontard! I wish your father and Mr. Brandio would hurry!"

# Early-Morning Swim • 9

IT WAS THIRTY or forty minutes longer before Mr. Wheeler and Mr. Brandio entered the small room where the Bob-Whites were waiting. A Secret Service man was with the two men. He was smiling. Trixie, watching, relaxed a little. Then, as she looked at Mr. Wheeler's serious face, her own sobered again.

"We've talked the matter over," the Secret Service man said. "We've checked your stories with these gentlemen. Much is involved. Many people, too, including the skipper of the boat that brought you all here."

*Then they do know that Bob may be mixed up with Lontard,* Trixie thought, and she listened carefully to what the Secret Service agent went on to say.

"Mr. Brandio explained how you were drawn into the case. We will want to talk to you further, perhaps several times. Young lady," he turned to Trixie, "it would be just as well if you worked *with* us in the future. Mr. Wheeler has explained your uncanny ability to hunt out infractions of the law. It's not a good business for two young girls."

Trixie straightened her back and tried to speak. The Secret Service man held up his hand. "I know, Trixie, that you and Honey have done some wonderful work as amateur detectives. This thing you're mixed up in now is pretty far over your heads. Why not let us take care of it from now on?"

"Trixie and I *never* hunt out cases," Honey protested loyally. "And we are going to have our own agency someday."

"Good! We can use all the talent we can get in this business. I didn't get into it myself till I finished college and law school. I guess I was about twenty-four years old when I got my first job in intelligence work. That gives you quite a few years to go, doesn't it?"

"Then, you think that if Honey and I see something that looks really suspicious, we should wait around till the police notice it?"

"Of course not! In our complicated society today, with all the projects that are under way—secret projects, projects that must be protected from subversive agents—we need the help of every citizen, young and old, in the United States. I don't intend to minimize the good you and Honey do, the good all the Bob-Whites do, or any organization like yours. I'm just asking you, Trixie, as a special favor to people whose lifework it is, not to try to go it alone. See what I mean?"

"I guess I do, sir. I didn't intend to go it alone, as you say. I was just waiting to see if there was anything we actually knew was wrong before I bothered Mr. Wheeler with it. Now I know you want us to report anything that even looks suspicious."

"Right you are. That's what the clerk in the Heartland Motel at Cairo was doing when he saw you take those papers from your purse. Don't hold that against him. By the way, girls, a word of warning: Don't mention those papers to anyone—not a word about them. Understand?"

"Yes, sir," Trixie and Honey chorused.

The Secret Service man turned around to the other Bob-Whites. "That goes for the rest of you, too, please. You'll probably hear from me again before long. In the meantime, I want you to all make a note of this telephone number." He wrote hurriedly on a card and handed it to Mr. Wheeler. "If any little thing comes up that seems to bear on this case, get to a telephone and let us know. I can't enlighten you beyond what you have seen and know, for until we appraise the papers, we can't get a clear-cut picture. If you're in any kind of danger, though, at any time —and we'll do our best to see that you aren't—call the nearest law enforcement group, then get in touch with us."

The Bob-Whites assured him that they did understand and would remember what he said.

"You aren't going to hold us any longer, then?" Trixie asked hopefully.

"No. We are releasing you to Mr. Brandio and Mr. Wheeler. We have told these gentlemen that we will want to be informed, certainly, before you leave this part of the country to return to New York. Don't forget what I've said, especially you, Trixie and Honey."

It was near dark when they left the federal office in downtown St. Louis. In the excitement, no one had thought about food. It was Mart who reminded them.

"Some of the rest of you may be able to live on air," he sighed. "Not me. I'm no hothouse plant. I'm starving. Let's find a hamburger joint, and soon."

Mr. Brandio smiled. "We'll settle for the Mayfair, just up the street, Mart. How about it? You can get

a hamburger in the *Hofbrau* there, if you insist, but
wait till you see the menu."

In the German restaurant, the crowd had thinned
out. The Bob-Whites eagerly gathered around a large
table, sniffing the good smells of German cooking.
Mart rubbed his stomach blissfully and, when the
waiter stopped for his order, ran his finger down the
page and said, "Bring me all of it, with a roast suck-
ling pig on the side."

When their food was brought, Trixie had no ap-
petite whatever. *Mr. Wheeler will start asking us a lot
of questions,* she thought, *as soon as we settle down
to eat. I can't answer any more. He's always been so
wonderful to us. He brought us here to St. Louis to
show us a good time. Now we've—I have, anyway—
embarrassed him in front of Mr. Brandio. I wish he
wouldn't look so worried.*

Just then Mr. Wheeler laughed out loud at something Mart said. Mr. Brandio laughed, too. Trixie's
heart took wings. Her plate in front of her had a new
and tantalizing look. Her mouth watered. A sigh of
gratitude to Mr. Wheeler and Mr. Brandio went up
from her full heart.

From that time on—as they ate their dinner, rose,
fully satisfied, from the table, and drove to the waterfront to pick up the car—Mr. Wheeler said no more
about their experience. Even when Trixie and Honey
rode to the motel with Honey's father and his friend,

Mr. Wheeler said nothing. At the door of the motel room he was brief.

"At Mr. Brandio's suggestion, I'll leave these two telephone numbers with you. One is a direct, unlisted line to Mr. Brandio's office, and the other is to his home. I'll see the boys and leave the numbers with them, too. I'll keep in constant touch with Mr. Brandio, and I can relay any information you give me to the police. One thing I ask of you: If you are puzzled about anything, telephone first and wonder about it afterward. In this case, please do as the Secret Service officer suggested: Work *with* them."

"Oh, I will, Mr. Wheeler, and Honey will, too, I know. I can't ever tell you how great I think you've been."

"Forget it. I think a lot of the Bob-Whites. I'm glad those papers are in the hands of the Secret Service agents. That should end the Lontard business. Good night, girls."

When he had gone, Trixie closed the door carefully and snapped on the night lock. Then she went to the mirror on her dresser and stood a long time, saying nothing, looking at her reflection but not even seeming to see it.

"What's the matter now?" Honey asked curiously.

"One thing I guess we all forgot. Your father did, apparently, and so did Mr. Brandio."

"What's that?"

"They took Bob off to the Coast Guard station before he knew about the Secret Service men questioning us. He doesn't know they were there or that they took the papers I had in my purse. If Bob doesn't know it, Pierre Lontard doesn't know it, either."

"So?"

"So he still thinks the papers are in my purse, doesn't he?"

"Oh, Trixie, you're right. Maybe we'd better call Daddy after he gets back to Mr. Brandio's and tell him what you've just said."

"No, let's not. We're safe inside our room. The door's bolted. The boys are right next door. It will be time enough to tell your father in the morning. I'm awfully tired, aren't you?"

"I am. I've just realized it. Tomorrow, though, we'd better tell Daddy. We have to do what the Secret Service men told us to do. And Daddy, too. That's why he left those numbers."

It didn't happen quite that way, however.

Trixie was sleepless. For a long time after she had said her prayers, she tossed from side to side. Her mind went back to the *Catfish Princess*, to the hootenanny under the stars. She thought of the ransacked room on the boat, of the man overboard, of the puzzlement and anxiety when the driver sent to meet them was detoured to Memphis, of the wild ride on the river with Bob, and of the session in the federal building in St. Louis.

Finally she fell into a deep sleep. It lasted about four hours. Unable to sleep again, Trixie sat up in bed. Dawn was breaking. Not a sound could be heard outside. The light over the swimming pool just beyond their window had been dimmed. She got up and pushed back the curtain. The dark sky, tinged with pink, was reflected in the water outside. The room seemed stuffy. The pool's coolness beckoned to Trixie. Quiet as a mouse, she slipped into her swimsuit, tucked a towel into her beach bag, softly slipped the chain from the lock, opened the door, and went out.

Faint stars and a pale crescent moon were still visible in the sky. Insects in the trees scratched out their ratchety music. On the highway beyond, heavy trucks went by, their noise somewhat deadened by the low motel buildings between the pool and the flower gardens and the road.

Trixie yawned, put her beach bag on the bench beside the pool, walked out on the board balanced above the pool, and dived cleanly into the cool, refreshing water.

She swam to the far end of the pool, climbed out, and sat on the edge, dangling her feet in the water. Then, in the half-light, at the end of the pool nearest the motel parking lot, she saw a dim figure emerge from the water and disappear. *Someone else likes to swim at dawn,* Trixie thought, *just as I do. The water feels so good.* Lazily she rose, walked out on the board, and dived gracefully down into the depths.

Before she could turn and head toward the surface, a strange, awful thing happened. Tremendous suction suddenly drew her toward the bottom. With all her might, Trixie fought, kicking hard against the concrete floor to force herself to the surface of the water. With every thrust, she was caught tighter in the whirling maelstrom that drew her murderously into its vortex.

The drain had been opened! Water was flowing with monstrous force through the outlet. Trixie was caught in its spiraling speed!

For a brief moment, her head rose above the water. Gasping, she caught a deep breath and screamed in terror. With renewed strength, she slashed the water, kicking desperately and flailing her arms. Using every ounce of strength, she fought her way out of the pull of the water to safety at the pool's edge.

There, summoned by her scream, the boys and Honey found her. Huddled around her, they soothed and reassured her. Honey held her dearest friend and smoothed her sandy curls. Color returned to Trixie's face. Strength slowly returned to her body.

"Somebody tampered with that drain," she said faintly. "I saw someone leave the pool as I swam to the far end. It was Pierre Lontard! I know it!"

"Oh, Trixie!" Mart protested.

"I'm certain of it." Trixie stood up. "He didn't wait long to close in, did he?"

"What could he gain by drowning you?" Mart wanted to know. "You seem to forget one very important thing. You've turned over the papers to the police. You're not quite yourself, Trixie, seeing things. . . ."

Trixie's eyes blazed. Her strength came back in waves. "You're the one, Mart Belden, who has forgotten the important thing. Bob was whisked away by the Coast Guard *before* I turned over the papers. Because he doesn't know, Lontard doesn't know. And, as for my seeing things, just look at that bench over there. I'm concerned because I'm *not* seeing things—things that should be there, like my beach bag. Pierre Lontard thought my purse was in it, just as sure as you're born. If I'm seeing things, where's my beach bag? Who but Pierre Lontard would want it enough to try to drown me to get it?"

"You win!" Mart said sadly.

"Let's wake the motel manager and tell him what's happened," Jim said, his eyes blazing.

"Let's get Daddy first," Honey insisted.

"Oh, not that . . . so soon!" Trixie begged. "He hasn't much more than gotten to sleep."

"None of us had," Mart said bluntly. "Why the

pool lured you out in the middle of the night, I'll
never know. Why couldn't you at least *act* like you
had some sense, Trixie?"

"That kind of talk won't get us anywhere, Mart,"
Brian said quietly.

"Nix on the criticism," Dan agreed. "Your sister's
had a bad fright."

"I know it," Mart said, trembling. "I'm still so
scared, I don't know what I'm saying. I just wish. . . ."

"I shouldn't have taken any risk right now," Trixie
admitted. "Mart's right about that. But how could
I know a swim would be dangerous? There's the manager now, so here we go on the merry-go-round
again! Mr. Wheeler to tell, the Secret Service to report to. . . ."

"And, in the meantime, where did Lontard go?"
Jim asked. "Halfway to the next state, while we stand
here gabbing. Here, sir!" he called to the red-faced
manager who hurried toward him. "You see, Trixie
got up early to take a swim . . . someone tried to kill
her . . . tampered with the drain . . . see where the
water level is now? The suction as the pool drained
almost drowned her. Isn't there a guard around this
place at night?"

"There is. Of course there is," the puffing manager
replied. "See here, suppose you begin at the beginning. What's wrong?"

# Off to Hannibal · 10

WHILE I'M EXPLAINING to the manager what happened, Honey, please get Dad and tell him about it." Jim's face was worried. "I wish these crazy things wouldn't keep happening."

"It's all my fault, all the time," Trixie said. "You might as well tell your father, when you talk to him, Honey, that I'm to blame for what's just happened."

"I won't tell him anything of the kind. You're not to blame. It's that man who's so desperate to get at those papers you had. I have to tell Daddy what happened, because we promised, and he'll have to report all this to the Secret Service, too."

"Well, get it over with," Mart told her impatiently. "I just hope he doesn't say we have to go back to New York right away. I'll die if I don't get to Hannibal to see the Mark Twain country."

"I don't believe what we want to do is important now," Trixie said sadly. "We've—that is, I have—interfered enough with the important work your father came out here to do. Maybe I didn't intend to interfere with it when I got mixed up with that Lontard, but now I'm so confused I don't know what I'm even saying. I'll go to my room and get out of this wet swimsuit."

"Will someone please take the time to tell me what this is all about?" the manager asked in a bewildered voice.

The boys told him, and he immediately summoned a maintenance man to check the drain in the pool. A few minutes later, the man reported that it had been opened—and not accidentally.

"So someone did do it deliberately," Brian said quickly, then lowered his voice. "It was Lontard, that's obvious."

Jim put his finger to his lips in warning.

"I get it," Brian agreed under his breath. "Mum's the word, till we talk to the police."

"What did you say?" the manager asked. "Did someone say something?"

No one answered, so he went on. "I don't understand any of this. I'm sure of one thing. No one deliberately tried to drown anyone. It's too fantastic. Why would anyone do a thing like that? Do you kids have any idea?"

"Trixie said a man ran from the pool just before she dived from the board, just before her accident," Mart said.

"A man ran from the pool? That couldn't be. She must have imagined it. My apartment is right in the front of the motel. I didn't hear a thing till the girl screamed. The restaurant is in front, too, and the pastry cook works at night—getting the baking done for the next day, you know. I'll ask him if he heard anyone or saw anyone."

"Here I am," the white-suited chef said. He had obviously been listening. "The kid's right. She really did see someone. I did, too. It was a guy in swim trunks, running for the parking lot. I opened the door to yell at him, but he gunned his car and drove off."

Trixie dressed hurriedly and joined the group in time to hear the cook's words. "Was it a black car?" she asked anxiously.

"All cars are black when it's dark outside," the cook said, grinning. "My granddad used to say, 'At night all cats are gray.'"

"Yes, yes, I see," the manager said impatiently. "It must have been some smart-aleck kid stealing a swim when he thought no one would see him. They'll do any kind of damage, these smart kids, wreck anything just for kicks."

"I don't think it was a boy I saw," Trixie said slowly and quietly.

"Whoever it was, I'll make it my business to find out. I'll put someone on it right away this morning. In the meantime, young lady, I'd better take you to the house physician. He must sleep like a dead man, not to have heard all this fuss. I want to know that you weren't injured."

"There's no need for me to see a doctor," Trixie said hastily. "I was scared, more than anything. I don't want to see a doctor. I'm all right. As soon as Mr. Wheeler gets here, we'll all talk to you again. In the meantime—here's Honey now—in the meantime, we'll go back to our rooms. I'm sorry as I can be that I was the cause of all this bother."

"I might, just as a warning, call your attention to one thing, Miss Trixie," the manager said sternly. "The hours for swimming are clearly posted above the pool. It may be a good idea if you observe them strictly in the future."

"I will. I will," Trixie said meekly.

"Boy, would you save us a lot of trouble if you were that humble all the time!" Mart remarked.

Honey bristled. "I like Trixie just exactly the way she is all the time. So there, Mart Belden!"

Trixie was still subdued when they lined up along the counter in the restaurant for hot chocolate.

"Daddy said he'd be here right away," Honey told them. "This is where he said for us to be, and he told us to get some hot chocolate. Trixie, your teeth are chattering."

"I guess I'm still nervous. I'm not cold. Was your father terribly angry at me?"

"Heavens, no! Did you ever know a time when Daddy was terribly angry at any of us? He was worried, and that's no surprise. He said for us not to move from this restaurant till he can get here. Do you really think that man you saw at the pool was Pierre Lontard?"

"I'm just as sure of it as I can possibly be. He really must be desperate, to do a thing like that."

"That's right. I don't see why the police don't arrest him right now. What are they waiting for?"

"Evidence," Dan said abruptly. "They haven't confided in us, but they can't just walk up to a man and arrest him, unless they have evidence. We don't know if they know where he is or what he's done."

"Well, I should think they have plenty of evidence," Mart said.

"No. There's plenty of suspicion, but that's not evidence," Dan insisted.

"Don't the police ever arrest anyone on suspicion?"

"Sure they do, Mart," Dan replied. "Sometimes

they get into some pretty bad messes doing that, too. Don't forget that Pierre Lontard is pretty smart. He might know that Mr. Wheeler is a millionaire. He may have destroyed any evidence that could convict him of whatever the police suspect he's done. Then he'd like to be arrested and sue Mr. Wheeler."

Mart wasn't convinced. "That sounds pretty unlikely . . . kind of crazy, really. I just hope they know where to pick him up when the time comes."

"If anyone is interested in what I think," Jim said, taking a long drink from a steaming mug of chocolate, "I think that we may be in on a pretty big case. It may even be an international thing."

"If the Secret Service men know so much, why did they let the Coast Guard take Bob off so quickly without questioning him?" Honey asked.

Trixie laughed. "With all the indictments they had against him, they knew where they'd find him when they got around to questioning him, didn't they, Honey?"

"Jeepers, I didn't think of that. I'm glad to hear you laugh, though, Trixie. My, but this chocolate tastes good. I'm hungry, too. We might as well order some bacon and waffles and eggs, don't you think? We have to wait right here for Daddy, anyway."

They were eating ravenously when Mr. Wheeler and Mr. Brandio came in. The early sun was shining brightly outside, and the motel was alive with morning activity. The coffee shop had begun to fill up. Mr. Wheeler took a stool next to Trixie. Mr. Brandio sat on the other side. "Tell us about it, Trixie," Mr. Wheeler said quietly.

Trixie's eyes lowered to her plate. She didn't answer. She seemed to be summoning courage to tell him.

"Speak up!" Mr. Wheeler urged. "Honey has told me, of course, that you went swimming in the pool before daylight, all alone. That was very unwise. You know that now, so I'll say no more about it. How you survive the dangers you get into, I'll never know. Honey told me of the drain. Just tell Mr. Brandio and me about the man you think you saw running away from the pool."

When Trixie had told them, Mr. Wheeler rose abruptly and went to the telephone in the corner of the coffee shop. The Bob-Whites watched him as he talked. They saw him nod, shake his head, listen for a long time, then place the receiver back on the hook.

"The man I talked with said he wished you were all back in New York. I must say I agree with him. If it weren't for the big meeting coming up today. . . ."

"Don't let that influence you," Mr. Brandio said hastily.

"Oh, please, Mr. Wheeler, we'll do anything you

think we should do." Trixie was contrite. "You don't
need to worry about me. I've certainly had my lesson.
Tell us what you think we should do."

"I do want to attend that meeting," Mr. Wheeler
said thoughtfully. "What would you think about
moving the Bob-Whites to another motel, maybe to
a downtown hotel, Mr. Brandio?"

Mr. Brandio considered the question for a while,
then said, "I'm not sure that would be a good idea.
The manager here will be more alert. He seemed
quite concerned when we talked to him a few minutes ago in the office. Of course, we can't tell him
about Lontard or those papers. . . ."

"Not without permission from the police," Mr.
Wheeler said. "They assured me, though, that they're
right on the job, and I'm sure they have their eye on
Lontard."

"They sure had their eyes closed last night," Mart
said.

"I guess they thought that, once we were locked in,
we'd stay locked in for the night," Trixie said. "I'm
sorry."

"Heck, we can find plenty to do right here at the
motel," Dan said, "if Trixie will agree to lay low and
not take any more risks."

"Oh, I will, Mr. Wheeler, I will. I'll be just as careful as I can be. We won't move from here till it's time
for us to leave for New York."

Mart groaned aloud and hit the counter with his fist. "I did want to go to Hannibal," he said under his breath.

"Hannibal?" Mr. Brandio repeated, his face lighting up.

"Oh, don't pay any attention to him, sir," Brian said hastily. "We sort of wanted to see Mark Twain's country, you know—where Tom Sawyer and Huck Finn used to hang out. Mart's been especially hipped on the subject, but that's unimportant now."

"I'm not so sure it is," Mr. Brandio answered. "Don't you see," he said to Mr. Wheeler, "they'd be miles from this area around the factories."

"How could they possibly go, after the rugged experience Trixie's had?" Mr. Wheeler was dubious.

Trixie interrupted hastily. "I'm fine! I'm just as good as ever. Nobody needs to worry one bit about how I feel. It never takes very long for me to snap back."

Mr. Wheeler smiled. "I should know that by this time. That isn't all, though," he said, turning to Mr. Brandio. "If Lontard followed them on the towboat, don't you think he'd follow them to Hannibal, too? No, I can't say it's a very good idea."

"After last night's episode, he'll take cover, I'd say," Mr. Brandio argued. "How about leaving it up to the police?"

"If Trixie feels equal to the trip to Hannibal, will

you be satisfied to have the police decide whether or not it is wise?" Mr. Wheeler asked the Bob-Whites.

"I'm sure we'd feel a lot better about going if the police knew about it and said it would be all right," Mart said hopefully. "Gosh, I'd sure like to go."

Mr. Wheeler went again to the telephone. He was smiling when he returned. "The man I talked with told me that, next to shipping you all back to New York right away, the best idea is for you kids to go off to Hannibal. He said you can make it easily in a day, have some time there, and be back before it's too late. Then we'll take off for New York tomorrow, with Mr. Brandio."

"Did he say anything more about Pierre Lontard?" Trixie asked.

"No, he didn't, but he did give me a special message for you, Trixie."

"You don't even need to tell me. I promised I'd not take any chances, and I won't. That's what you were going to say to me, wasn't it?"

"Substantially, yes. He put it a little plainer. He said to tell you again to please let the police handle the case from now on . . . that if they wanted your cooperation—that is, the cooperation of the Belden-Wheeler Agency—they'd ask for it."

"He needn't have said that," Trixie answered unhappily.

"Stick close to us, and we'll see that you remember what he said," Mart told her. "Shall we get going? I've got the map all marked, Jim. It's a straight shoot north from here. Boy, am I glad we're going! This motel is jinxed. I'll be glad to get away to where there's some fun—Jackson's Island—the old cave! Huck Finn, here we come!"

They said good-bye hastily to Mr. Wheeler and Mr. Brandio and all crowded into the car. With Jim at the wheel, they rounded the curve from the airport and headed south to Bypass 40, then turned directly north on Highway 79. For the moment, they seemed to have forgotten the events of the early morning.

Mercifully, they didn't know what still lay ahead of them.

# Surprise at Jackson's Island • 11

Wasn't it good of Mr. Brandio to let us take this car?" Jim said as he guided the little automobile along the busy highway. "We sure wouldn't have been able to get very far without it."

"He's been great!" Mart said as he squirmed to find more room in the backseat. "Boy, this car wouldn't carry another pound, would it?"

"Only six people in it?" Trixie said, laughing. "Why, back home we've crowded more than that into a car."

"Not if they weighed as much as Brian and Dan."

"You know where you'd be sitting now if Diana could be with us? I miss her so much!" Trixie sighed, then settled back in her seat.

"Since I'm the youngest, I'd be out on the hood, I guess," Honey chuckled. "There or back of the rear seat, up against the window. I wish Diana could be here, too. We could use her. She can almost read people's minds at times, can't she?"

"We could sure use a mind reader right now," Brian said solemnly. "I'm about as much in the dark as a person could be about Pierre Lontard and those papers."

Trixie spoke up thoughtfully. "Do you know something? I wish we'd made a copy of those papers."

"How did we know they were going to be taken away from us, silly?" Mart answered. "Anyway, who'd want the old things?"

"The police," Dan answered sharply. "What would you want the papers for, Trixie? I think we're better off to have them in the hands of the police. It isn't so dangerous."

"You mean it wouldn't be so dangerous for us *if* Lontard knew the police have them. He still thinks they're in my purse, though. I'd at least like to have that map of the Mississippi, with those queer sketches. I *know* they mean something. I didn't have the papers long enough to study them carefully."

"I still think the police'll come up with egg on their

faces," Mart insisted. "They'll find they've been chasing up a blind alley. Nothing much has happened lately, has it?"

"Nothing much except that Trixie nearly drowned," Dan said with sarcasm.

"That didn't have to be Lontard's fault. Even the manager thought it was some crazy kid who monkeyed with the drain."

"You believe what you want to believe, Mart, and I'll believe what I want . . . and I have absolute faith in the Secret Service."

"Why not? You're going to be a policeman yourself someday. Anyhow, you know more about the Secret Service than any of the rest of us."

"You're right about that," Jim said. "Why don't we forget the whole business for today? Dad and Mr. Brandio, and the police, too, were glad we were going to be away from the airport area for a day."

"Yeah, and we'd better get back in time to see some of that exhibit the airplane factories are getting ready for the big brass from Washington," Mart said. "If we have to leave tomorrow, I'd like at least to get a squint at a space capsule. What do you think they'll say at school if we tell them—"

Brian laughed out loud. "That's the argument you use about everything."

"It's how I get to see almost everything. Anyway, we should be able to get around a bit in Hannibal—

see most everything we want to see—and still take in the exhibit tonight."

"That's the old spirit, Mart," Jim said. "Let the police handle Lontard and the rest of that business from now on. Let's forget it. How about it, Trixie?"

"I don't *want* to let the police handle it all by themselves. That's no way for our agency to act, is it, Honey? Honey and I are the only ones, as far as I know, who've really seen Lontard. I doubt if the police can handle it without us."

"They're going to have to, Sis," Mart said. "We're out of communication today, I hope. Then tomorrow we fly back to New York."

"I don't care. I don't like it, that's all."

"How about forgetting it for today, at least?" Jim asked good-naturedly. "Is it a deal?"

"I'll try," Trixie said grudgingly. "We're sure making time on this wide highway, aren't we?"

"Uh-huh. We're already more than halfway there," Jim replied. "Is anyone hungry?"

"I am!" Mart shouted.

"That's chronic," his brother remarked.

"But even if I am, I'd like to wait till we get to Hannibal," Mart went on. "There's a cafe in the Becky Thatcher house. It said so in the article we read about Tom Sawyer's hometown. It was in the *National Geographic*, remember? I'd like to eat there. I'll bet they serve the same things they ate in

Hannibal in Tom Sawyer's day."

"Like the bats Injun Joe ate in the cave?" Brian asked.

"How do you know a bat wouldn't taste good?"

"Ugh, I hope I never find out," Trixie said, shivering. "It'll be fun, though, to eat in Becky Thatcher's house. Part of it is a library, I think. Hundreds of thousands of people must visit Hannibal every year, and all because of Mark Twain's stories."

Mart grunted. "What I'd like to do would be to see some of the things tourists don't get to see."

"We won't have time to hunt out anything that isn't on a regular tour," Jim told him. "Just be grateful you'll have a chance to see any of it."

"That's Sunny Jim talking," Mart said sourly.

"And it makes a lot of sense," Brian told him. "You can't cover the whole waterfront in a couple of hours. Didn't that last road sign say we're pretty near Hannibal, Jim?"

"We should be there in about twenty minutes, if the going's as good as it has been." Jim took a right turn on a small country road. "This one will take us right along the river. Gosh, the Mississippi is wide out there. It looks as though there's no current at all. Lots of good fishing places along here. There's a kid ahead of us with a fishing pole."

"From the back he looks just like Huckleberry Finn," Trixie shouted.

Honey touched Jim on the shoulder. "Let's slow down and talk to him."

"Yeah," Mart agreed. "Maybe he can give us the lowdown on where to go and what to see."

Jim pulled the car over to the side of the road. "Hi!" the Bob-Whites called out.

The boy swung his fishpole over to the other shoulder and walked up to the car. "Hi! Where you from?" When they told him they lived in New York, he exclaimed, "Well, I'll be a catfish! Come all the way in that car?"

Jim laughed. "No, we didn't. We all think you look just like Huck Finn. You aren't, are you?"

"Huh-uh. I ain't even his ghost. But if I ain't Huck Finn, I was born and raised right here on the river near Hannibal, an' I know every inch Huck and Tom traveled when they was here."

"You do?" Mart asked eagerly. "Could you show us? How about coming along with us up to town? We haven't had anything to eat. We'll buy your lunch at the cafe in Becky Thatcher's house. Can you come?"

The boy's face lighted. "I don't care if I do. But how can you stuff another person in this car 'thout a can opener?"

"I'll show you," Mart answered, and he squeezed far back into the corner. "Have a square inch or two," he said, waving airily to the space beside him.

When the Bob-Whites told the boy their names, he repeated each one, then said, "I'm Lem Watkins. As I told you, I live right here on the river. My dad works down on the wharf. I've got three brothers. They work there, too. Say, are you awful hungry?"

"Not exactly starving," Trixie answered. "Why?"

"Well, it's this way. If you'll slow down a mite, I'll show you the road that leads over to the cave—you know, that cave where Tom and Becky was lost . . . where old Injun Joe died. Would you like to see it? Wouldn't take you more'n part of an hour. Yeah?" His face was covered with a freckled smile. "Then turn here!"

Jim followed Lem's directions and stopped the car near a triangular entrance to a big cave. A number of other cars were parked there.

"Tourists!" Lem said disgustedly. "You have to pay to get in. I forgot to tell you that. It's the only thing you have to pay to see in all the Mark Twain places. You see, a man bought it from the city, an' he has to charge admittance to get his money back. You don't have to pay for me. I can wait here. If you did get me a ticket, though, I could sneak you around to some places they don't let tourists into."

"It's a deal!" Jim said, and he counted out the price of admission for all of them.

A guide was just starting down one of the long corridors with a group of sightseers. Lem ignored him and beckoned to the Bob-Whites. "Come over this way."

"This here's Aladdin's Palace," he told them as they entered a huge cathedral-shaped room hung with glittering stalactites. Its walls were frescoed in candle smoke, with the names and addresses of thousands of visitors. In the far end of the big room, a miniature Niagara cascaded from a small spring that crept in between layers of limestone. Lem took his candle and walked back of it, illuminating it just as Tom Sawyer had done to impress Becky.

All around them, bats flew in and out around the thick columns of crystal stalagmites. Honey cringed, remembering the bats in the frightening Ozark cave they had visited the summer before.

"This here's the bench where Tom an' Becky sat when their candles give out an' they almost starved to death," Lem said. "They don't let everybody in here now. They used to, but people got lost. I wish they'd never put all them electric lights around. A long time ago, we used to really have fun here. Want to see some more?"

"No," Honey and Trixie said in one breath.

"It's the bats," Honey added. "They scare me. Missouri must have a lot of caves. We saw so many of them in the Ozarks."

"The state's chuck-full of 'em," Lem said proudly. "Now, I could show you another about a mile from here. Nobody owns it, an' we can go as far in as we want."

"I guess not, thanks," Jim told him. "We haven't too much time to spend in Hannibal. Right now, I guess we'd better go and get something to eat."

Disappointed, Lem apparently didn't think he'd earned the ticket they had paid for at the cave entrance. "Shucks, you'd have to stay a month to really see anything. Tell you what. I got an idea. How'd you like to go over to Jackson's Island and build a bonfire and cook our lunch? I got a raft right down in the willows. We can cross over in a jiffy. I do it all the time. When we get there, we can catch us some fish. My raft's got pontoons on it," he added proudly. "It can carry an army."

"Hooray!" Mart shouted. "We can stop at a grocery store and get some stuff."

"Just bread an' eggs an' maybe some bacon to sop the bread in," Lem said. "I got me a fryin' pan over there, an' some tin cups. There's a spring nearby, I mean nearby where I'm goin' to take you. How about it?"

"Let's go!" Brian shouted. They all piled into the car.

"Don't you think we'd better at least drive by Tom Sawyer's house?" Dan asked.

"And Becky Thatcher's?" Trixie added. "And the famous fence?"

"That's the house right over there." Lem pointed it out. "That's the museum next to it, with a whole lot of things from Mark Twain's day, like a big paddle wheel from a steamboat." Lem's eyes glowed. "An' right alongside of the museum, you can see the fence Tom Sawyer whitewashed . . . right there . . . ain't it white, gleamin' in the sun? They whitewash it twice a year."

Trixie gasped and put her hand to her mouth.

"What's the matter?" Jim asked, slowing the car. "Did you see someone?"

"No," Trixie said soberly, "it's the teeth. Don't you see? It's the teeth!"

"Have you lost your marbles?" Mart asked, leaning over from his perch in back. "What do you mean by 'teeth'?"

"That drawing we thought looked like teeth on that map of the Mississippi River. That map Lontard seemed so worried about. Why didn't we know it was a fence instead of teeth? That fence is the most famous thing in this town, I guess."

"It really is, Trixie." Mart whistled. "My, but you're smart. Out in the river, beyond the fence, there was a sketch of an island."

"Jackson's Island!" Brian snapped his fingers.

"Golly!" Mart said admiringly. "We've just *got* to get over there now."

Trixie nodded vigorously. "I honestly believe we're

on the trail at last. The fence and the island were the topmost sketches on that map of the river. That could mean it's the end of the trail."

"Or the beginning," Jim said.

"If we get over there, we may find out," Mart said. "What's holding us up? Let's get to a grocery store and then to the raft!"

Without even a thought of the promise they had made to the police or to Mr. Wheeler, they piled onto the big old raft. It was hidden among the willows at the foot of a street that led to the river's bank.

Lem pushed off, jumped onto the middle of the raft, and grabbed a long pole. Mart, grinning from ear to ear, took the pole on the other side.

"I ain't had so much fun in a long time," Lem said. "We'll fry us some fish an' fry us some bacon an'. . . . Say, hanged if I know what you meant when you was talkin' about teeth."

"Forget it!" Mart said. He poled manfully as Lem guided the raft skillfully across the river and up onto the white, sandy, island beach, where he fastened it to an oak stump.

"You gather up some wood," he ordered, "an' I'll get a mess of fish. Start fryin' up the bacon, girls," he called back as he disappeared into marshy underbrush.

For an hour the Bob-Whites lived in a world of pioneers. The island was deserted. It was as primitive as it had been when Tom Sawyer (The Black Avenger), Huckleberry Finn (The Red-Handed), and their friend Joe Harper (The Terror of the Seas) had walked its sandy shore.

After they had scoured a long-handled skillet with river sand, Honey and Trixie fried thick bacon and heaped it on a plate of oak leaves. They had hardly finished, when Lem arrived from his secret fishing spot with two fat bass and half a dozen small catfish. With his many-bladed knife, he cleaned and scaled the bass, then skinned and slit the catfish. Then he quickly popped them into the bacon fat.

While the girls were preparing the bacon, the boys had been off in the blackberry bushes that covered the island. They returned with briar scratches but triumphantly holding two large cans filled with plump, juicy blackberries.

What followed was the best feast the Bob-Whites could ever remember. They were ravenous, for they hadn't eaten since very early morning at Vacation Inn.

When they finished, they scoured the pan and gathered up the debris. Then they sat around the fire, waiting for it to get low enough to "stomp out," as Lem said.

"Doesn't anyone live on this island?" Dan asked Lem. He put his hand over his eyes and peered back into the woods.

"Nope—leastways nobody who has a right to. This place is federal property. Nobody's allowed to come here, really; but the police, they don't mind if kids come, long as they behave theirselves."

"It looks like a good place for a hideout for criminals," Dan offered. "Is anything hidden back there in the woods?"

Lem's eyes narrowed with suspicion. "Whaddya mean?"

"Don't you ever run across anything that looks like a place where crooks have been? It seems to me strange things could happen back there . . . maybe murder. Don't you think so, Mart?"

Mart nodded. "I guess strange things never happen here, though."

"Then you guess wrong," Lem said. "If you'll promise never to tell a livin' soul, I'll tell you what I seen with these very eyes just last week."

The Bob-Whites quickly crossed their hearts and promised.

"Well, me and Soapy—he's my best friend—we was campin' back yonder." Lem pointed his thumb toward the woods. "Long about midnight, Soapy was asleep, and I was jest droppin' off, when a boat slid onto the sand out there."

The Bob-Whites leaned forward, all ears.

"I watched three fellas get out of the boat an' drag a big bundle after 'em. I was so scared I thought my teeth would rattle outen my head. Soapy, he didn't wake up. They put one bundle down an' went for another. I thought it was about time for me to let Soapy know what was goin' on, 'cause sometimes he talks in his sleep. I thought if they heard him, it would be good-bye for us. I whispered real low till I woke him up. Do you know what that dumb clunk did?"

"What?" the Bob-Whites shouted.

"Grabbed his rifle from under his blanket an' let it go! You coulda heard it clear to St. Paul, Minnesota. Was I scared? I'll say, but not half as scared as them fellas. They dragged the bundle back, heaved it into the boat, grabbed their oars, an' hightailed it out of here like a bear was after 'em."

"You never found out who they were? You never found out what was in those bundles?" Trixie held tight to Lem's arm and gazed into his face.

"No, ma'am, I never did. The onliest thing I ever found was this. Wait till I git it." He went off into his secret place in the woods and came back with a soiled envelope. Out of it he drew a piece of paper and handed it to Trixie. She took one look at it and passed it around to the other Bob-Whites, without a word.

It was a sheet of graph paper covered with scraggly lines—a blood brother to the papers Lontard had left in the wastebasket, the papers now in the hands of the Secret Service.

# St. Peter · 12

WHERE DID YOU find this paper?" Trixie asked, her voice excited.

"Layin' smack on the sand, right there. I didn't pay any attention to it at first; then Soapy said it looked like pirates' writin'. This is our pirates' lair." Lem swept his hand to include the woods back of the beach.

"May we *please* look at the pirates' lair?" Trixie begged. "It's terribly important."

"No, ma'am. That's somethin' I couldn't let you do. You see, we promised in blood, us pirates, never to let anybody see our lair. I don't know what they'd do to me for jest tellin' you this much. I guess we better git out of here now."

Trixie was persistent. "Can't you just lend us the paper, then, for a little while? We'll honestly see that you get it back."

"No, I can't do that, nuther. That paper belongs in our chest. I don't know now why I ever told you anything. Why are you so nosy? I guess I told you in the first place 'cause I thought anybody from way off in New York wouldn't pay any attention to kids here on Jackson's Island. Let's git out of here, right now!"

"What we want to know is pretty important to the whole United States," Dan tried to explain. "How about letting us have a look back there?"

"No, sirree! Never! Supposin' you'd find out some of the secrets us pirates got. Don't you never tell nobody 'bout that paper or 'bout the pirates or 'bout them men we seen. Remember, you promised before I told you. Remember?"

"Yes," Trixie admitted unhappily. "I remember. We haven't seen your pirates' lair, so we can't tell anything about it. I *do* wish we could take one look."

"Well, you can't," Lem said, herding them toward the raft. "An' don't get any ideas about sneakin' back here, either. Soapy's rifle ain't the onliest one we use to guard our lair. So keep out! Come on, let's git goin'. I gotta get home, or I'll get a hidin' from my ma."

It was late afternoon when the Bob-Whites turned the crowded car toward the airport and their motel. At Trixie's suggestion, they agreed to return to St. Louis by another route. Trixie thought they might discover other places to remind them of the sketches on the river map.

"We'll have to hustle along, or we won't get back to see that space exhibit," Mart reminded Jim. "It looks like rain, too—all those clouds. This is no short-cut along the river. I don't know why you had to stick around that island for so long, Trixie. You sure didn't dig up any information."

"I did, too, Mart Belden. What do you say about that paper Lem found?"

"What good will that do you, when you promised not to tell about it?"

"That's right. We did find out, though, about those men going ashore with those bundles."

"You can't tell that, either. We promised. Anyhow, I don't think it had anything to do with Pierre Lontard—not if you think he was stealing plans from one of those airplane factories. He couldn't carry a space-ship in a bundle."

"Mart, you're always suspicious about everything I try to do, every clue that Honey and I find. Of course they couldn't carry a spaceship in a bundle. That's silly. That paper *did* belong with the other papers of Pierre Lontard that I found. As far as the bundles are concerned, they could contain models. Experts make models of spaceships before they start to build the real thing."

"Of course, Trixie," Dan agreed. "And they make thousands of parts. Those men could have some spaceship parts in the bundles."

"Then, please tell me why they'd have to take them as far north as Jackson's Island and park them there," Mart insisted. "I'd say you're sniffing on a trail that just isn't there."

"They'd want to hide them as far away as they could, till they had all the stuff accumulated. The bad part of it is that I can't tell Mr. Brandio or the police anything about it. Why did I have to promise?" Trixie looked out at the fast-gathering clouds on the horizon and sighed.

Honey gazed into space, and she sighed, too. "It was the best clue we've had, and we can't use it."

"Or can we?" Trixie's face glowed. "We can at least do this: We can tell the police to check everything on that map of the river very carefully, and we can say that we're sure the sketches mean something."

"Maybe we can do that ... maybe," Honey said. "Jeepers, it's getting dark, isn't it?"

"The wind's coming up, too," Brian said. "Let's speed up, Jim. There's not much traffic on this side road. You should be able to make good time. Not much chance of clues along here, either, Trixie. We made a mistake to come this way."

A terrific gust of wind hit the car, and lightning flashed across the black sky, almost blinding Jim. The car swerved onto the shoulder of the road and almost upset as Jim jerked it back onto the pavement.

Then the rain came, first in large drops pounding against the windshield. Then the sky seemed to open and spill tons of water all at once.

"We'd better find some sort of shelter!" Brian shouted. "Not under these trees by the side of the road, Jim. Lightning might strike them."

"I . . . know . . . that," Jim said, tugging at the wheel to keep the car under control. He strained his eyes ahead. "Isn't that a side road? It sure is. I'll pull up there. We won't be in danger of anyone running into us, at least. Gosh, it's dark. Look at it pour!"

The light car found traction in the gravel of the side road and slowly forged ahead. Trees thinned out, and a dark mass loomed ahead.

"It's a private road we're on," Brian muttered. "That looks like a house. Boy, is it a big one! Almost as big as your house at home, Jim."

Honey shivered. "I'm glad we don't live in such a spooky place. Isn't that a porte cochere on the side? We could pull up under it, couldn't we?"

"Sure we can, Sis," Jim said. "You must have eyes like an owl's. I can hardly see a thing. I only know I'm still on the road."

"You're on the driveway and almost under cover," Trixie cried. "Stop, now! There!"

"Jeepers, that's a relief!" Jim took his hands from the wheel. "This is worse than a storm in the Catskills. I thought nothing could beat one of those."

"The wind's blowing so hard it may blow the old house over on us." Honey snuggled down in her seat. "I'll bet it's been ages since anybody lived here."

"I'm just glad nobody's home," Mart said. "Imagine the characters that would live here—witches and goblins and . . . gangsters. If you're looking for a hideout for Lontard's outfit, you couldn't find a likelier place, Trix."

"It's the lightning and thunder and rain that make it look so scary," Trixie declared. "I don't remember anything on the map of the river that would make us think Lontard uses this place."

"Nope. Me, either," Dan said. "Let's see what we can remember about those sketches. There was that fence at Tom Sawyer's home, and there was Jackson's Island. That figures, especially after we saw that paper Lem Watkins found. I wish we had it to show to Mr. Wheeler."

"Then there was the picture of pyramids," Honey remembered. "That was Cairo, I guess."

"I don't know why they'd have Cairo on the map. It was made—the map, I mean—long before Lontard was mixed up with us Bob-Whites," Brian said.

"Well, there was a picture of a fez, too," Trixie said. "I have it! It meant Thebes—fez and pyramids. Remember how Bob tried to take the *Comet* into shore at Thebes?"

"Golly, yes," Brian said. "The fishermen scared him out! I'm beginning to think there really *is* something to that crazy map."

"I've always been sure of it," Trixie said smugly.

"Remember the old man with the beard? Bushy beard? You know, like one of the prophets in the Bible?" Dan recalled. "We haven't seen anything like that yet."

"No, we haven't, but there were sketches at intervals on the river, from Hannibal to New Orleans," Trixie said slowly. "Those sketches were one reason I wanted to follow a road near the river. We might possibly run into the old man. Maybe he's a hermit and lives in this old house."

"If he does, he's going to live there in peace, as far as I'm concerned," Mart said determinedly. "The rain's slackening a little. Let's get going, Jim. I want to see that exhibit."

"Jeepers, Mart, that's probably rained out. I think it's much more important to keep hunting for Lontard's caches," Trixie said.

"There's a chance it wasn't rained out," Mart insisted. "The sky's all light down south of us. It's black as night here. Say, come to think of it, it *is* night.

We couldn't see a clue if it walked up and slapped us on the back. I want to see that exhibit. I think we'd better pull out. Jim, are those headlights coming up the road?"

"Looks like it. They've just turned off the county road and are coming this way. I'd better scram."

"Oh, don't do that!" Trixie begged. "We're just on the brink of finding something out. I'm sure of it. This old scary house. . . ."

"That's good reason for us to get out of here," Brian said with authority. "Pull out fast, Jim."

"It's too late now. Maybe I can back out. I can pull around to the rear of the house and hide the car, maybe, back in that grove. Hold on, everybody!"

Jim backed skillfully, turned the car around, and headed for the grove. He was fortunate to find cover without any trouble, for he couldn't use his lights. Then they all sat, without a word, watching.

The car sped up the drive and stopped under the porte cochere. Three forms got out quickly and climbed the few steps to the carriage entrance.

The Bob-Whites strained their eyes to catch a glimpse of the three persons, but in vain. They disappeared into the house so quickly that they were just a blur of murky shapes.

Flickering lights appeared as the visitors went up to the second floor, then the third. There, a single bulb, just visible through an uncurtained window, showed a barnlike, apparently vacant room.

"I'd say this is our time to get out," Mart said, "when they're all inside the house."

"Just what I was thinking," Brian agreed.

"And me." Jim turned the ignition key.

"Oh, Jim, don't go away now, please," Trixie begged. "I just know we're on Lontard's trail."

"And I know we're going to get a dose of shot in our backs if we don't get off private property," Mart said. "Trixie, you sure do go in for wild guesses. This is someone's home, and we're trespassing. The quicker we get out of here the better, if we want to save our hides. Right, Jim?"

"Right!" Jim stepped hard on the gas.

Trixie was crushed. As the car sped down the driveway and out toward the road, she looked back longingly. Suddenly the house was ablaze with light. Doors were thrown open, shadowy shapes ran out to the waiting automobile, and soon the big car's motor roared.

"Hurry!" Mart urged. "Give her more gas, Jim!"

"I'm hurrying. This is as fast as I can go," Jim shouted.

"Then it isn't fast enough. Listen to that baby roar! They'll be on us in a minute. Turn off the road, Jim!"

"What do you think he's doing?" Dan cried.

Jim slid the car down a small incline and took cover under the trees.

The big car, its lights glaring, tore past the hidden car and out onto the county road, went around the corner on two wheels, and roared off down the highway.

The Bob-Whites sighed with relief—all but Trixie. Her puzzled gaze followed the dark bulk of the big car till it disappeared. Then she shook her head as though to clear her thoughts and said determinedly, "Now's our chance to see what's going on back in that big house."

"Are you crazy?" Mart answered. "If you think Lontard has anything to do with that old house back there, tell it to the police. It's their job. I don't have to remind you that we promised not to take any chances. And, obviously, the people who live there don't like company. *I* say leave it to the police. How about it, gang?"

Even Honey agreed with Mart. "I doubt if that house has anything to do with our case. We just happened to get into somebody's private estate, and they wanted to find out who we were, that's all."

"Maybe so," Trixie said reluctantly. "That car that passed us . . . I wonder! Do you have any idea where we are, Jim?"

"Not the vaguest."

"There was a sign where we turned off the road. That is, I think I saw something that looked like a sign. Where's the flashlight?" Trixie asked.

Jim passed it over his shoulder to her, and as the car rounded a curve to the county highway, Trixie flashed the light around. Sure enough, there was a sign. Trixie read it silently. When its significance struck her, she read it again, aloud and triumphantly: " 'St. Peter'! Now, what do you think of that?"

"Not a thing," Mart said, disgusted. "How about letting us in on what you're gloating about?"

"St. Peter!" Trixie repeated excitedly. "It's as plain as the nose on your face. It's another one of those stopping places on Lontard's map. Remember the old man with the beard? St. Peter, of course!"

Mart laughed derisively. "Of all the far-fetched ideas I've heard, Trixie Belden, this one takes the cake. St. Peter! I seem to remember that there was a picture of a steamboat with the picture of the old man. Probably an old steamboat captain, instead of St. Peter. St. Peter is a town."

"Well, all I can say is this: You wait and see, Mart, and all the rest of you, too. If you'd only gone back to that house, maybe we could have found out what the picture of the steamboat meant. Maybe there's an old steamboat on the river back of the house. You wait and see!"

"Maybe there isn't, too," Mart laughed. "I'd like to see your face when you tell all this junk to the Secret Service men."

"You won't have a long wait," Trixie said, settling

back in the seat. "We're going to talk to them in the
morning, before Mr. Brandio's plane takes us back
to New York. I think you'll be laughing on the other
side of your face."

Suddenly a thought struck her. She remembered
the shape of the big car that had passed them. "Yes,
sirree, Mart Belden, you'll be laughing on the other
side of *your* face. Did you happen, by any chance, to
notice what kind of a car that was as it passed us?
Did you?" Trixie's voice rose confidently. "Did you?
It was a Mercedes. I'm practically positive."

"Golly!" Mart said, awed. "You could be right,
Trix. Golly!"

# The Aguileras Again · 13

IT WAS LONG after seven o'clock when the Bob-Whites returned to their St. Louis motel. The rain had stopped, and the air was cooling.

"Nobody'd ever think we almost drowned in a rainstorm not fifty miles north," Mart said. "It didn't any more than sprinkle here. Am I glad of that! It means the exhibit at the airplane factories wasn't rained out. Get a place to park fast, Jim, and let's get going. Can't we drop the girls and go right on from here?"

"What do you mean 'drop the girls'?" Trixie asked indignantly. "We want to see the exhibit, too. If you'd only think, you'd realize that there'll be lots of girls among the future astronauts. How do you know Honey and I may not want to try it someday?"

"I can imagine *you* orbiting the sun, all right. It's a little harder to imagine Honey doing it."

"Where Trixie goes, I go, too," Honey said. "The Belden-Wheeler Agency will probably have lots of cases in outer space."

"That may be so," Brian told her. "Tonight I think it's a good idea for you to stay home. You almost drowned at dawn, and we had quite a day at Hannibal and in the cloudburst on the way home."

"I'm no baby," Trixie insisted. "I'm not a bit tired. We'll clean up a little and get something to eat in the restaurant. Then Honey and I will go to the exhibit, too. Who knows? We may pick up something terribly important there."

The Bob-Whites piled out of the car and went into the motel. As they passed the desk, a clerk gave Jim several messages that had accumulated during the day.

"Most of them are from Dad," Jim said. "I guess he's been trying to find out if we were back home and if we want to go to the exhibit. All the notes say is for me to call him."

"We were going to do that, anyway," Trixie said. "We have to report what happened today. If he thinks it's important, he'll pass it on to the police, I guess. He'd be sure to do it if we could tell him about the paper Lem found. I wish our agency could do more to help on this case. It really is *our* case, and now the police have taken over, and we don't even know what's happening. Are you going to call your father, Jim?"

"Right now. Let's call him from my room. I may need the rest of you to fill me in on some of the facts."

While Jim talked, the Bob-Whites crowded around the telephone.

"Yes, Dad. . . . No, Dad. . . . Yes, I think so. . . . No, I'm telling you about it just as it happened. . . . I can't tell you just why Trixie thinks Jackson's Island is hooked up with Lontard. She's certain of it, though."

The Bob-Whites could hear Mr. Wheeler laughing heartily.

"I might say the rest of us are pretty certain of it too, Dad. We're pretty sure of one thing: It *was* Lontard on that county road. . . . Mercedes, yes. Well, Trixie wanted to go back and investigate."

The Bob-Whites kept quiet as Jim told the story. They seemed on edge as he went over the details.

"We *didn't* let her go back to the old house. We knew you wouldn't want her to do it. . . . Yes, she was all worked up about that crazy map of the river which had the sketches on it. She's sure that the old man with the beard was St. Peter—the old man on the map. The sign we saw said 'St. Peter.' It was right near the old house. . . . Yes, Dad, here she is."

Trixie took the telephone. As she talked her face clouded and reddened; then her mouth sagged. "I'm not tired. I'm just as rested as anybody could be. I rested in the car coming back. Yes, Mr. Wheeler. I see, Mr. Wheeler. Well, I guess I'll have to, then."

When Trixie relinquished the receiver she was provoked. "You could have told him, Jim, that I'm all right. Now I can't go with all of you to the exhibit. I know I should be there. You'd think I was an old woman of sixty and had to go to bed with some sassafras tea or whatever it is they give old ladies. I wish my father could be here." She stamped her feet angrily. "He'd let me go."

"I don't think he would," Honey told her. "My dad lets us do just as much as yours does. You know that, Trixie."

"Yeah," Mart said, "and if Dad did weaken and let you go, Moms would veto it pretty quickly."

"I suppose you're both right. I'm sorry I spoke as I did. I hate to pass up the exhibit. I wish I could go."

Honey put her arm around Trixie. "I'm not going if you don't go. It isn't that important to me. We can pick up a magazine at the coffee shop. We can watch television, too, while the boys are off at the exhibit." The girls walked slowly to their room.

"You don't have to stay here because of me, Honey. I don't want you to do that. If you want to go, please do."

"I don't want to go. We can write up an account of everything that's happened so far on this case. That can be useful to the Secret Service men in following up the case after we go back to Sleepyside."

Trixie opened the door to their room. "I *wish* we didn't have to give up the case and turn it over to the police."

"The telephone's ringing. You answer it, Trixie. It's probably the boys calling to tell us to hurry over to the coffee shop."

"Shhhh!" Trixie held up a warning finger. "It's the police."

Apparently the police were checking on Mr. Wheeler's report of the day's happenings, because they asked Trixie to tell them, in detail, everything that had occurred from the time they arrived in Hannibal. She told them about the teeth that turned out to be the fence Tom Sawyer once whitewashed. She reported their visit to Jackson's Island. She couldn't tell them of Lem's account of the men he and Soapy saw in the night, but she did say she thought Jackson's Island was a very important link in the chain. Then she told what happened on the way home, stopping frequently to give Honey a chance to add to the story or to corroborate something she said.

After Trixie finished talking she said to Honey, "I honestly think the police are beginning to think we're right, Honey, and that this is an important case.

"That policeman asked me about every little thing. I was afraid he'd question me more about the island, but he didn't. I know Mart wasn't much impressed with the old house part of it. . . ."

"He was when the Mercedes passed us."

"That's right. He was. The policeman seemed to think it has real bearing on the case. I guess it's a good thing I'm not going to that exhibit, after all, much as I'd like to go."

"Why?"

"Because the policeman said he may have to communicate with us further, after he's talked to the rest of the men. He asked me if I'd be available later on."

Outside the girls' room, the Bob-White whistle shrilled.

"That's Jim," Honey said. "They probably want us to hurry to the restaurant. Are you ready?"

At the counter Trixie admitted, "I'm famished and I didn't realize it. I thought I'd never be hungry again, after all that fried fish and bacon and eggs on Jackson's Island. Did you ever taste such fish in all your life?"

"We get some pretty good fish in the creek in our woods back home," Jim said, "but they don't taste like the fish Lem caught."

"There aren't any catfish in our creek," Mart lamented. "At least I never saw one there. Did you get Lem's address so we could write to him?"

"I did," Trixie said. "It's a good thing I did, too, because when I talked to the police they said they wanted it."

"When you did what?" Brian shouted.

"You haven't given me a chance to tell you that the police called me about what happened today. *You* thought none of it was important, Mart."

"I never said any such thing, especially after the Mercedes. Boy! Tell us what the police said, Trix."

So Trixie brought them up to date. As she ended her story, she was conscious of Honey's nudging. "What's up?" she asked curiously.

"Look who just took a seat over there in the corner," Honey whispered. "Pass the word along to the boys. It's Mr. and Mrs. Aguilera, isn't it?"

At that minute Mrs. Aguilera caught sight of the Bob-Whites seated along the counter. She got up, and her husband followed.

"Honey! Trixie!" she cried, hugging them both. "We're so glad to see you! We got here this afternoon and tried to call your room a while ago, but there was no answer. We thought you were probably off sight-seeing. Aren't you surprised to see us here?"

Trixie, quickly recovered from the first shock of surprise, answered, "Well, *I'm* surprised certainly.

I guess the others are, too. Did anything happen to the *Catfish Princess?*" Her voice was anxious.

Mrs. Aguilera laughed. "Oh, no. Something happened to us. When we stopped at Memphis, there was a letter there waiting for us—"

"How did you get here?" Trixie broke in.

"I'm coming to that, Trixie," Mrs. Aguilera said indulgently. "You see, my husband and I are writing a book about rivers— But then, I told you that a long time ago on the towboat, didn't I?"

"Get to the point, Elena!" her husband said impatiently.

"Yes, I'll do that. Give me a minute. The letter at Memphis was from our publisher. He said we must bring the work up to date immediately, then return East for another assignment. I guess he thought we were having too good a time traveling up and down the Mississippi. He should have had to cook for all those people!"

"Then how do you happen to be here at this motel?" Trixie wanted to know.

"You don't sound very pleased, Trixie," Mrs. Aguilera said, irritated.

"Oh, I am . . . I think . . . well, I think it's swell."

"I think it's wonderful," Honey added quickly. "I'm so glad to see you again. Trixie was only surprised. That's why she sounded the way she did."

Jim leaned over past his sister and asked quietly,

"Just how *did* you happen to come here, Mrs. Aguilera? We're curious."

"Yes, we are," Honey repeated. "We did hope we'd see you again sometime, and now it's happened. Tell us about Captain Martin, Deena, and Paul."

Mrs. Aguilera hugged Honey again. "Thank you, dear. I did look forward to seeing all the Bob-Whites again. Deena and Paul both sent messages to you. Captain Martin, too. He said to tell you he'd found out who ransacked your cabin. It was one of the new deckhands. Captain Martin put him off the boat at the next stop after Cairo. But that's an old story. First I must tell you why we are here at the motel. It's really your fault."

"Our fault?" Brian asked, raising his eyebrows.

"In a way. My husband's manuscript and my pictures and films were in such disorder that we felt we had to find a place to stay for at least a day or so, to put things in order before going East. . . ."

Mr. Aguilera seemed to come to life as his wife talked. "So we remembered what you'd said about this place near the airport. It seemed to be just what we were looking for, and here we are."

"Did you fly here from Memphis?" Trixie asked.

"No. Fortunately we had left our car at Memphis. It was the place where we stopped first on the river when we came from the East. I took quite a lot of pictures around there, and my husband made notes.

We rode north with a friend who had business in St. Louis, hoping to take a boat down the river, pick up our car again in Memphis, and maybe go on down to New Orleans. We were fortunate to get jobs on the *Catfish Princess*."

"It sounds kind of mixed up," Mart said, "but I hope you like it here at the motel. We do. At least, I guess we'd like it if we were ever here long enough to find out. Here comes our food."

"Then we mustn't interrupt you further," Mrs. Aguilera said, taking her husband's arm. "Perhaps we'll see you tomorrow?" she asked the girls.

"Oh, yes," Honey said quickly. "That is, I guess maybe we will. We're going to fly back to New York tomorrow."

"On what flight?"

"No regular flight. We came out here as Mr. Brandio's guests. He owns one of the airplane factories here. We'll go back on his private plane, whenever he gets ready to leave. I'm sure we'll see you in the morning, though."

"How about tonight?" Mrs. Aguilera persisted. "We could have a little talk this evening, maybe?"

"We're going to be away this evening," Dan said. "Sorry."

"We're not!" Honey sang out. "That is, I mean Trixie and I aren't going to the exhibit of spaceships with the boys."

"I guess you don't remember *why* you aren't going," Dan reminded her. "Mrs. Aguilera, it's because Mr. Wheeler thought Trixie should get to bed early."

"Oh, of course," Honey said. "You see, Trixie almost drowned in the pool early this morning—"

"If you'll excuse us now," Trixie said abruptly, "we'll go on to our room. We undoubtedly will see you in the morning. Have you finished eating, Honey?"

"No, not quite. What's the big hurry?" Honey asked. "Mrs. Aguilera, we will see you and your husband before we leave. And if you're ever in New York or just passing through Sleepyside-on-the-Hudson—"

"Do look us up," Trixie said, trying to make her voice cordial. "Good-bye for now."

The Aguileras returned to their table, and the boys went on to the exhibit. Honey and Trixie went to their room.

"I must say you were awfully high-handed with Mr. and Mrs. Aguilera, Trixie." Honey's face was red. "You could have been a little nicer, without half trying."

"I didn't mean to be 'not nice,' as you say. I don't happen to like either one of them."

"That's no reason to be so uppity. You might try remembering that Mrs. Aguilera practically saved your life on the *Catfish Princess*."

"I wish I were as sure of that as you seem to be. I don't trust her, somehow or other. I'm not even sure she didn't push me, back there on the towboat, nearly knock me overboard, and then make it look as though she had saved my life."

"Why, Trixie Belden, I never heard of anything so insane in all my life. Why would she do that?"

"I don't know. I feel it in my bones. When I feel anything in my bones, I can't help the way I act."

"I'll say this much, then. I'm pretty good at guessing what people are like, too, and I'd trust Mrs. Aguilera anyplace. You're not acting like yourself."

"Maybe I'm not. Maybe she's all right. Maybe she's won all the medals there are for being trustworthy. But I don't like the look on her face when she's talking to us."

"Go ahead, then. Think what you want to think. As far as I'm concerned, I think they're both awfully nice people, though Mr. Aguilera never has much to say. I don't know many people who can write books or take pictures to illustrate them. Maybe they'll put us in their book."

"Oh, Honey, let's quit talking about the Aguileras. When we don't agree on something, we usually agree to disagree. Let's turn on your transistor radio. We can get some music to make us sleepy."

"I don't need anything to make me sleepy. I

shouldn't think that you would, either, after all you've been through today." Honey yawned.

Trixie took the hint. She crept into her twin bed and turned off the light. The transistor on the table between them was turned low; it was playing dreamy music. Soon Trixie was aware of Honey's rhythmic breathing and knew she had fallen sound asleep. She listened a little longer, then snapped off the radio and turned on her side.

A soft light from the pool area filtered through the Venetian blinds at the window. It was past closing time at the pool. There was not much sound from anywhere, except the occasional noise of an automobile as it passed far out in front of the motel area.

Trixie couldn't sleep. All the events of their stay in St. Louis and their trip down the river went through her mind. She tried to fit the pieces of the puzzle together, but she couldn't. *I've never been so mixed up,* she thought. *Anybody would know that something terrible is going on, but I can't figure out what it is.*

A shadowy figure crossed in front of the curtained window. Then another. No, the same one going back again, trying hard to be soundless.

Trixie, instantly alert, sat up in bed, her eyes turned toward the window. From somewhere nearby she heard whispering. Then the bell at the door tingled.

She slipped into her skirt, blouse, and loafers, then aroused Honey. She waited till she dressed to open the door and discover their caller.

Mr. and Mrs. Aguilera stood there.

"We're sorry to awaken you," Mrs. Aguilera apologized, "especially since you need rest so badly, Trixie."

"What is it? Has something happened? Is anything wrong with the boys?" Trixie's words fell over one another.

"No, it isn't that," Mrs. Aguilera said hastily. "I must hurry to tell you, for we haven't a minute to lose. Someone has been lurking outside your window, and my husband and I have waited for a chance to knock at your door without being seen."

"Yes? What has happened now?" Trixie asked. "Don't keep us in suspense."

Mrs. Aguilera smiled and handed Trixie a folded note. "It's from the police."

"The police?" Trixie asked, completely dumfounded.

"Yes. Didn't you guess? I was sure you knew by this time that my husband and I have been working with the Secret Service. Read it quickly!"

Trixie held the paper under the floor lamp and read out loud:

"Trixie: Since I talked with you earlier this evening, things have happened pretty fast. Our agents, Mr. and Mrs. Aguilera, will explain to you what I mean. Please obey without hesitation what they ask you to do. Your life may depend upon it. Trust Mr. and Mrs. Aguilera. They are protecting you."

The note was signed "Leighton N. Ogilvie, Chief of Secret Service, St. Louis District."

# A New Development • 14

A STRANGE LOOK of unbelief crossed Trixie's face as she read the note. Without a word she passed it on to Honey.

"Then you really are on the police staff?" Trixie asked slowly.

"There! See?" Honey said, thrusting the note back into Trixie's hands. "I told you so. I always knew she was someone special."

Mrs. Aguilera laughed indulgently. "I wanted to tell you many times, Trixie, but I didn't feel free to do so till the chief said I could reveal who we are. You

must trust us now," she added hurriedly, "and go
with us. We must hurry. We're pretty sure the men
who've been lurking around your part of the motel
are on their way now to their rendezvous. What they
don't know is that the police have it surrounded and
that when you girls arrive, you'll be able to identify
at least one of them. You know who. Come with us
quickly!"

"Oh, yes, of course," Honey said, taking Mrs.
Aguilera's hand. "Isn't it exciting, Trixie? We're really
going to solve this case before we go back to New
York. That's what we wanted most to do. Now,
thanks to Mr. and Mrs. Aguilera—"

"Just a minute, Honey. Mrs. Aguilera, I want my
brothers and Dan and Jim to go with us wherever we
go. They went to the exhibit of spaceships over on the
airport grounds. They'll be home very soon."

"I'm sorry. There's not a minute to lose."

"We have to get going," Juan Aguilera insisted.
"Hurry! The car is over on the side lot. We can get
out this way, right here between these motel units."

"Well, maybe if the girls would rather wait till the
boys come . . ." Mrs. Aguilera began, but her husband silenced her with one word.

"No!"

Mrs. Aguilera's hesitation, her willingness to wait
for the boys, lessened Trixie's feeling of apprehen-
sion; still she persisted. "I'd at least like to call Mr.

Brandio's home to leave word for Mr. Wheeler. I want him to know where Honey and I have gone."

"He'll be at the rendezvous. Both he and Mr. Wheeler will be there, you may be sure of that, by the time we get there," Mrs. Aguilera said to her soothingly.

"I'd like to try to reach him, if you don't mind," Trixie said determinedly.

"Make it quick, then," Mr. Aguilera said.

Trixie took off the receiver and waited for the dial tone. Nothing happened. She clicked the mechanism. There was no sign of life on the wire.

"Hurry!" Mrs. Aguilera warned.

Trixie clicked again, then hung up the receiver. "The line's dead. I'll have to go to the office and use the phone there."

"There isn't a moment for you to go anywhere," Mr. Aguilera said.

"Then I'll leave a note for the boys."

"Make it snappy!" Mr. Aguilera commanded. "We've already wasted too much time. Write it out on this piece of notepaper. I'll put it under their door while you go with my wife to the car."

Trixie scribbled a quick account of what had happened. She told the boys that she didn't know where they were going, but it looked as though the case might be settled very soon, that they'd been surprised to find that Mr. and Mrs. Aguilera were working with

the Secret Service, and that she had tried to telephone to Mr. Brandio's house, but the line from their
room was dead. If the boys would call the Brandio
number right away, they'd surely find out more information.

Trixie would have written more, but both of the
Aguileras were urging her to hurry. Honey, too,
seemed impatient and eager to get on the way.

When she had finished writing, Mr. Aguilera held
out his hand. Reluctantly Trixie gave him the folded
paper. "I could easily put it under the door myself,"
she said under her breath.

As the girls went out to the waiting car, Trixie
could not get rid of a lingering feeling that something
was very wrong. Why hadn't the police at least hinted
that these people were in their confidence? Why did
she have this feeling of actual dislike for Mrs. Aguilera? Honey, however, seemed to accept the new de-
velopment as something legitimate, and Honey was
pretty good at analyzing people.

Both girls sat in the back of the big black Cadillac,
one on either side of Mrs. Aguilera, while Mr. Aguilera stepped hard on the accelerator. Then he backed
and turned, with all wheels whining as they spun on
the gravel.

"Where are we going?" Trixie asked. "We're head-
ing north, aren't we?" She peered into the darkness,
looking for some familiar road sign.

"I really don't know," Mrs. Aguilera said serenely. "I don't bother about such details when my husband is doing the driving. I'm one of those silly women who know absolutely nothing about automobiles. You aren't old enough to drive, are you, Trixie?"

"No, I'm not, but my father lets me drive up and down our driveway. I can handle a car. I know how to start and stop and back up and. . . ." She leaned over to try to see the speedometer. "I know we're going awfully fast now. What is the speed limit in Missouri?"

Mr. Aguilera didn't answer. He growled something unintelligible.

"He never talks to anyone when he's driving," his wife explained.

"He doesn't talk much any other time, does he?" Honey asked, laughing. "I guess he keeps his mind on his business. Have you been in detective work very long?"

"Years," Mrs. Aguilera answered, "in one form or another. Trixie seems to be a natural-born detective herself."

*Oh, don't let Honey tell her we* are *detectives,* Trixie prayed, and her prayer was answered. Her friend started to speak, then smothered her voice with a cough. She was silent after that.

The speeding car passed everyone on the road, weaving in and out of traffic skillfully and surely as it sped northward in the dark night.

Trixie was almost sure they were on the same road their car had followed on their return from Hannibal. That seemed a million light-years ago. Oh, if the boys were only with them now!

As the car passed another familiar place along the highway, Trixie grew more and more apprehensive. Ahead of her a junction of two highways loomed. Red and blue neon lights indicated a filling station or, perhaps, a roadside cafe.

"Mr. Aguilera," Trixie said purposefully, "please stop the car at this junction ahead. I want to try and telephone back to the motel to tell the boys where we are."

"No."

"He means he hasn't time now," Mrs. Aguilera explained.

"I just *have* to telephone to them," Trixie insisted, "because we have promised one another always to report our whereabouts. I *must* telephone," she repeated, her hand on the door. "It's right ahead now. You have to stop at the junction, anyway. I'll rush the call through. It won't take five minutes."

"No." Mr. Aguilera hesitated only a second at the stop sign, then put his foot down hard again on the accelerator.

"Why, Trixie," Mrs. Aguilera said in a soft voice, "I do believe you may still be distrustful. Surely that note from Chief Otway should have convinced you that we are friends—"

"Chief Otway?" Trixie repeated, terror shaking her voice. "The name on the note was Ogilvie. I remember it well."

"Of course!" Mrs. Aguilera trilled. "There was an officer called Otway. How silly of me. Ogilvie is the chief's name. James N. Ogilvie."

"The note said 'Leighton N. Ogilvie,'" Trixie said in a weak voice. "Did you hear that, Honey? 'Leighton N. Ogilvie'—not 'Otway' and not 'James N. Ogilvie.' Did you hear that, Honey? Did you?"

"Yes, I did," Honey answered. "I heard it. It would be a hard name to remember, Mrs. Aguilera."

"Shut your traps, the whole bunch of you!" Mr. Aguilera called savagely. "That means you, Elena, too. Of all the dimwits I've ever known, you're number one on the list . . . can't even remember your own name. Hold tight, dear young ladies, for I'm slowing down to turn!" He whirled the steering wheel to the right and reeled into a dirt road.

Trixie shaded her eyes and looked into the darkness. She was sure she saw the arm of a sign and sickeningly sure that it said "St. Peter." They were back on the road that led to that old house! The Aguileras were going to stop there and maybe kill both her and Honey. Something terrible was bound to happen. Involuntarily she reached across Mrs. Aguilera's lap to find Honey's comforting hand.

On the car went. Not quite so fast now, for the dirt road was narrow and the shoulders were high. A dense wood closed in on each side. The bulk of the old house lay ahead in the darkness.

"Why are you taking us here?" Trixie asked, scarcely able to form the words, for cold terror gripped her. Her mind went back to the map of the river, the map that was among the papers Lontard left in the room at the motel. *They're following that same route*, Trixie thought. *They're in cahoots with Lontard! That's certain!*

"Where are we?" she asked again defiantly, her voice stronger. "Why are you taking us here?"

A low growl answered her from the front seat, and Mr. Aguilera glanced back.

"Because this is the road that leads to the rendezvous we have with the police," Mrs. Aguilera answered slowly. "If you will be patient, you will find that out in a very short time now. We are nearing our destination. Try to trust me, Trixie."

"That awful old house!" Trixie cried. "We're near it. We're going to stop *there*, Honey. We're going to stop there, and I just know something awful is going to happen to us."

"We're not stopping there!" Honey sang out confidently. "We've passed it. Mrs. Aguilera would never let anything bad happen to us."

It was true that they had passed the house. They were back of it now, on a bumpy trail overhung with branches. The Cadillac nosed its bulk slowly through the thickening vines and came to a stop.

"Get out!" Mr. Aguilera ordered.

"We must walk from here," his wife said soothingly. "It's not a very good path, so watch where you're going. We're not far from where the police and the others are waiting. I'm sorry you're going to get your feet wet."

"We don't mind that," Honey said.

*It's only a lark for her,* Trixie thought resignedly. *Heaven only knows what's waiting for us. I'm glad Honey isn't suspicious. What good would it do us if she were?*

Mrs. Aguilera gave Honey's arm a squeeze. "Don't be afraid. Very soon now you will see your friends. Just think, you'll be in on the solution of a very big mystery!"

In spite of herself, Trixie's heart quickened. There was a bare chance . . . but no! The old distrust returned with increased intensity.

No one had a flashlight but Mr. Aguilera. They followed his steps closely, thrusting aside vines and bushes, stumbling, almost falling, as they went blindly along.

From the murky distance ahead of them, there were the sounds of late birds settling for the night.

Trees rustled, and bare branches over their heads rubbed their ghostly arms together. Silence, silence— except for the sound of their own groping feet as twigs crackled and broke beneath them.

There was a peculiar smell in the night air, a pungent smell of rotting vegetation and deadwood. It was a familiar smell— Willows!

"We're near the river, aren't we?" Trixie asked. "Is that where everyone is going to meet us? Are we really going to meet Mr. Wheeler and the rest of them?"

"Of course we are, Trixie," Honey assured her. "This is scary, though, isn't it? It's so dark. I hope we'll get there soon."

Mr. Aguilera strode ahead, his big feet sloshing loudly in the increasingly marshy ground. He flashed his light from side to side and down at the ground in front of him. "Watch out for snakes!" he called.

Honey cried out in terror. "I'm deathly afraid of snakes!" She stopped, unable to move another foot.

"Now you've done it," Mrs. Aguilera called to her husband. "You've scared Honey so she can't even move. We'll have to carry her."

"Carry her?" Mr. Aguilera repeated, laughing. "I can just see myself carrying one of those brats. Give her a good hard kick. That'll boot her ahead, all right."

"He . . . didn't . . . mean . . . that . . . did . . . he?"

Honey asked, trembling all over.

"Of course he didn't. He's just anxious to get to where we're going. There aren't any snakes here, anyway, and you don't need to be afraid. Here, take my hand." Mrs. Aguilera grasped Honey's arm and drew her forward, forcing her to lift her feet and follow along.

As Honey faltered, Trixie's mind darted quickly from one thing to another. She thought of the first meeting with Lontard at the motel and how his piercing dark eyes bored through her. She remembered the menacing bulk of the Mercedes as it crowded their helpless car on the highway—helpless till Jim's quick recovery eluded the car bearing down on them. Oh, if the boys were only with them now! She remembered how she had almost stumbled into the river from the barge far in front of the *Catfish Princess*. She recalled the thieves in her stateroom and the person she saw swimming away from the towboat. It certainly was Lontard.

She remembered the false message sent to Mr. Wheeler from Cairo, the way Bob had acted on the *Comet*, and the landings he had attempted to make. She remembered the one he *did* make, with the Coast Guard in pursuit.

She remembered, shivering, her struggle in the swimming pool and the man who disappeared as she sat on the edge of the pool.

She thought of Jackson's Island and the evidence Lontard had left there. Everything clicked into focus, even the car that roared onto the highway as their car left the old house.

Now here they were, right back on the same road, and ahead of them a watery death in the river!

"There's an old boat!" Honey cried as the trees ended in a great open space. "It's the Mississippi River and an old steamboat, Trixie! Now, that's where we're going to meet my dad and all the others. Did they come by boat? Why didn't we meet them and come by boat, too? This is a terrible way to come to the old steamboat. My feet are soaking wet, and I'm so cold and scared. . . ."

"That won't bother you much longer," Mr. Aguilera snarled. He pushed the two girls up the old plank to the main deck of the dilapidated steamboat.

"Go on!" he ordered. "Up the next steps to the pilothouse! Go on. Move faster."

"The others?" Honey asked, stumbling ahead and reaching back for Trixie's hand. "Aren't they here yet?"

"Oh, yeah," Mr. Aguilera chuckled. "The others are here, all right. Open up, Frenchy!"

A huge light flashed on the deck above.

Trixie and Honey, shaking and faltering, walked the few steps across the top deck to the pilothouse. As they neared, rusty hinges creaked, and the door swung wide into a dimly lighted room.

There, his feet planted far apart, rocking back and forth on his heels, stood Pierre Lontard. He was exultant; a grin covered his face.

# On the Steamboat • 15

GREETINGS, MY DEAR little detective friends!" Lontard said, his voice as oily as that of Red Riding Hood's wolf. "Aren't you glad to see me?"

Trixie and Honey could not answer.

"Well, aren't you? You've played cat and mouse with me for far too long. So you thought your dear friends Elena and Juan Aguilera were protecting you from me!" He laughed again, a deep, throaty, evil laugh that sent Trixie's blood racing cold to the very tips of her fingers.

Honey was deathly pale.

"What do you intend to do?" Trixie asked with superhuman courage. "What do you want from us? Are you going to kill us?"

"One question at a time, my pretty little spitfire. First, what do I want? My papers you stole from me and which you still keep from me. I want those immediately. Search her thoroughly!" he commanded Mrs. Aguilera.

"Then, for the second question, what am I going to do to you? Am I going to kill you? The answer to that question depends entirely on you, Miss Trixie. For your companion, I do not care, except that what happens to you must happen to her, too, for she has a tongue.

"In my country to steal private papers means certain death to a thief. In your country, men are more compassionate. Perhaps I have learned compassion from your people, yes? What have you to report, Elena? You have found nothing?"

In the light of the huge battery-charged lamp, Trixie could see the contents of her purse strewn on the floor.

"Nothing!" Mrs. Aguilera repeated.

Pierre Lontard turned furiously on Trixie. "Where are they? Where are the papers?" He gave her such a shove that she nearly fell to the floor.

"I . . . do . . . not . . . have . . . them. . . ."

Suddenly Honey rushed to him and scratched him

furiously across the face. Half blinded by her attack,
he swung on her and would have struck her, but Mrs.
Aguilera stepped between them. "Wait," she commanded. "We do not yet have the papers."

"That is right. We do not. Where are they?" he
demanded of Trixie in a cold, hard voice. "Answer
me, miss, immediately. Beware of what will happen
to you if those papers are not returned! You have cost
me thousands of dollars already, evading me and
withholding from me my rightful property. Where
are they?" He stood over Trixie, arm upraised, waiting for the answer.

"Don't you see she doesn't have them?" Honey
answered. "How could she? They're—"

"Honey, no!" Trixie cautioned. "Let me talk,
please."

Honey put her hand over her mouth and nodded
pitifully.

"Then speak!" Lontard howled in fury. "Speak!
Where are my papers?"

A thought raced through Trixie's mind. *If I tell him
now that the police have the papers, he will certainly
kill us.* Her voice never faltered as she said bravely,
"I can say nothing except that I don't have them.
They are no longer in my possession."

"That is very plain. Where have you put them?
Where have you hidden them? Speak immediately,
or take the consequences." Lontard's voice was filled

with rage, and his face reddened.

"I have said all I can. I do not have them."

"Then you have hidden them. Where?" He swore fiercely. "Now I must go and find where you have hidden them. Very well. *If* I do not find the papers where they are almost certain to be—in your room at the motel—then, my pretty little Trixie, you will no longer be pretty. Bind her! Take care of both of these interfering meddlers! Never mind gentleness, Elena! Think what they have done to us! Think what their actions have cost us!"

"Don't you dare touch Honey!" Trixie cried. "She had nothing to do with the papers. I don't know what they mean, but they must be terribly important and very dangerous to make you do what you're doing. Don't you dare touch Honey!" she cried again as Mr. Aguilera seized Honey's arms.

"Silence!" Lontard ordered.

"You'll be sorry for what you're doing!" Trixie warned. "If we're hurt, our parents will track you down to the far corners of the earth."

At this Lontard laughed again, wickedly and cruelly. "Then let your parents find you. They will look for you, maybe, in the weeds of the river down there, eh?"

Honey cried out pitifully, "Oh, Trixie, do tell them where to find the papers. They'll kill you! Oh, Trixie!"

"Trust me, Honey," Trixie begged. To Lontard she

said, "You're far too smart to think you'll go unpun-
ished. Our relatives and friends will never rest till
they hunt you out."

"Find me?" Lontard laughed sarcastically. "You
weak, cowardly Americans couldn't find the letter A
in the alphabet. You're a bunch of spineless idiots."

"You can't say that!" Trixie shouted defiantly. "If
you dare to touch us, to harm us, you'll suffer all the
days of your life, and they'll be few and short."

"Let them go!" Mrs. Aguilera said. "I've been in
this country longer than you have, Pierre. I know
the penalty for kidnapping ... and for murder!"

"You evidently do not know, or have forgotten, *my*
power and who is behind me," Lontard answered
coldly. "*I* am afraid of no one. I am Pierre Lontard!
As for letting them go, have you lost your mind? We
would abandon everything we have worked for. Is
that your wish? We would give up all we have
planned, all we have risked lives and fortunes to ac-
quire. Is that what you want now? Faugh!" He spat
contemptuously.

"Even if you do not care for the fortune that is
waiting for us," he went on scornfully, "what about
our lives? With two smart girls like these alive, how
far could we get? Nowhere. No, Elena Aguilera, pro-
ceed! Waste no more time. Keep your pity for yourself. You make me sick! Let them go? When did
Lontard ever do that? Never! Tie them! Gag them!

We must get going immediately."

Mr. and Mrs. Aguilera, spurred on by Lontard, seized the girls, crossed their arms behind their backs, and bound them. Then they pushed them roughly to the floor and tied their ankles together.

This done, they rolled the girls over and bound their mouths. "There! Is that satisfactory?" Juan Aguilera asked his master.

"It will keep them from interfering for a while," Lontard said grimly. "Perhaps forever. Much depends upon what we find, and how quickly we find it, at the motel. We must go immediately. There is always the danger that the boys may have tried to communicate with the girls after the exhibit was over. You can still hear what I am saying, young ladies. I shall give you one last chance to tell me where the papers are, or you will be left here until it is our desire to return. Nod your head, Trixie, if you are ready to talk to me."

Trixie did not move.

Lontard took out his watch. "I shall wait sixty seconds for your answer."

Trixie did not move.

"Speak, girls," Mrs. Aguilera pleaded. "Make some motion that you will do as he asks. He can be very cruel."

Neither Trixie nor Honey moved.

Lontard counted the seconds with a motion of his

long forefinger, then, with a growl, clicked shut the cover of his foreign-looking watch.

"Now you deserve no consideration, and you will get none. Come!" he told his confederates. He put out the flash lantern and pushed Mr. and Mrs. Aguilera ahead of him through the door. Outside, the rusty key scraped ominously as Lontard turned it in the lock.

Trixie could hear quick steps descending the rickety stairs and walking across the plank to shore, then nothing. No sound. No light. No hope. Nothing but black darkness.

Bumping her bruised body, Trixie tried to move herself closer to Honey. She mumbled through the tight gag, and Honey mumbled back. In this way she was able to locate her friend and finally to feel her nearness. There was some comfort in that.

Through the cracked and broken windows of the pilothouse, Trixie could hear the lapping of waves against the low-hanging willows.

Out on the river, there was nothing but silence. In the marsh around them, a fish occasionally jumped and fell back into the water, the splash echoing and reechoing.

Gradually, on shore, animals that had been frightened by the presence of Lontard and the Aguileras took courage again from the silence and continued their stealthy hunt for food, making small, unfamiliar noises. Muskrats swished through the grasses, hunting clams, cracking them with a snap, and sucking their rubbery flesh. The peeping of small tree frogs rose shrilly above the bass *arrumph* of bullfrogs.

Trixie, listening, struggled mightily at the cords that held her. She rolled over and pushed her back against Honey, hoping that maybe Lontard had left at least one of her friend's fingers free to work at the knots.

Honey seemed to sense her intent, but if her hands were not as closely bound as Trixie's, they were so numbed by the pressure of the cord that they were useless.

Back in her throat, Honey made strange bleating noises, but if they meant anything, Trixie could not interpret them. She answered, though, with glugging moans, for any human sound in the great black void gave her courage.

From up the river, a towboat whistled mournfully, and far off, on the Illinois side of the river, another boat answered. As it slowly made its way downriver, the boat threw its searchlight from shore to shore. *Surely they'll see this old wreck,* Trixie thought. *But what good will it do us? It's probably been rotting here for nearly a hundred years.*

Gradually the light from the towboat disappeared, and the floor under the girls rocked in the wake of boat and barges.

*If only I could talk to Honey!* Trixie thought. *If only I could tell her why I couldn't tell Lontard where the papers are. I know she thinks I should have told. She doesn't realize that I was trying to save us from sure death, once he knew the police were on his track. On his track?* Trixie's heart quickened. Could the police possibly know about the Aguileras? Know the whereabouts of Lontard? If they did, perhaps. . . . No, the time was too short now for any help to come. When Lontard had searched their room in the motel without finding the papers, he would return immediately, dispose of both of them in some frightful way, and then be off.

Frantically Trixie's mind explored every possible source of hope . . . and ended in a blind alley. There seemed nothing to do but accept, numbly, the fate that seemed inevitable.

In the darkness that followed the passing of the towboat, Trixie heard again the furtive rustling of animals and birds outside. Slowly, too, she became aware of sounds nearer to her. She raised her head. In the corner of the old room, she could see bright pinpoints of eyes that glittered in the faint moonlight. Then she heard the scurry of little feet and the squeaks of hurrying mice. She bumped her body to frighten them away. Honey must not know they were there. She was so afraid of mice. Slowly, hopelessly, she realized how unimportant this was, in the face of the more horrible things they now had to fear.

The mice, frightened by her movements, soon disappeared. Stillness came again, absolute stillness. A cloud passed over the moon and blackness surrounded Trixie and Honey. Finally, exhausted emotionally and physically, the two girls slept.

# A Key · 16

Daylight was reaching through the shattered windows of the pilothouse when Trixie awakened with a start. Honey, close to her, didn't move.

Trixie had been dreaming—a horrible nightmare. She was glad to awaken and find her dream just a dream. Then reality swept over her, and she realized that no nightmare could be worse than the thing that was actually happening to her and Honey.

When she tried to move, her body would not respond. The tight bonds had slowed her circulation, numbing her arms and legs. *I must move,* she thought, *and I must move Honey*. Summoning all her strength, she threw her body feebly against Honey's. Her friend stirred, awakened, realized where she was, and moved her body closer to Trixie.

Trixie was surprised that Lontard and his accomplices had not yet returned. She well knew that the time would soon come when they would know the fate that was in store for them. Her first waking thoughts were prayers for help.

The sun was just coming up. There was no sound from the shore except the stirring of birds in their nests. There was no sound on the river. Towboats must have tied up for the night, and fishing boats had not yet appeared.

Trixie was aware of extreme dryness in her throat. She longed for water. She was not hungry, but the vision of a glass of clear, cool water haunted her. Honey must be very thirsty, too.

Since the moment of awakening and her small movement toward Trixie, Honey had not stirred. Maybe she had fainted! Trixie bumped her body against her friend's. Honey answered with a low moan from the back of her throat.

Sustained by the thought that Honey was alive and conscious, a little of Trixie's courage returned. She raised her head and looked about. In the early morning light, she could see signs of her captors' recent activity. Empty cans from soup and baked beans

were collected in a corner. There were chicken bones
on the floor along with discarded milk cartons and
empty wine bottles.

The floor near the girls was strewn with torn paper
and scattered tissues. Trix saw the broken mirror of
her compact there, too, glistening in the morning
light. Nearby lay her address book, and on the floor
near her purse, where Mrs. Aguilera had hastily
thrown it, lay the key to their room at Vacation Inn.
By some queer chance, not one of the three had
noticed the key.

*What a fool I was ever to come here with the Aguil-
eras!* Trixie thought tragically. *It was bad enough
for me to take a chance, when I always suspected
Mrs. Aguilera's motives. It was worse for me to in-
volve Honey. Now we'll never again see our homes in
Sleepyside. Mr. Wheeler will think I even deserve to
die, because I will have caused Honey's death! Oh, I
do wish my dad could know where I am. And my
moms. I'll never see my little brother Bobby again!
Where can the boys be? Can't they know how badly
we need them? Jim, where are you? Brian, Mart,
Dan? I'm sure something would tell me if they were
in danger. They're sleeping, safe in their room at the
motel.*

Trixie concentrated with all her might on trying
to send a mental message for help. Try as she would,
she couldn't feel she had reached the mind of any-

one—the boys, Mr. Wheeler, Mr. Brandio, the police.

Gradually, in the midst of her thinking, Trixie became aware of voices. On the shore somewhere she could hear faint voices. They were young voices. Mart? Dan? Brian? Jim? The voices came nearer. She could hear words. The voices were those of strangers, but someone alive and near was speaking, someone who wasn't Pierre Lontard, who wasn't the Aguileras!

Trixie alerted Honey. Both girls raised their heads to listen.

"I sure would like to get that old bass," a boy's voice said.

"I've got dibs on that old fish myself," another answered. "I saw him first. Why'd you suppose I got up so early?"

"To get here before I did," the first one answered, laughing. "I caught you, though, didn't I, just as you stepped out of your yard?"

There was a sound of crackling branches pushed aside and the sloshing of rubber boots through marshy grass.

"There's bass enough here for both of us. Over there on the other side of that log, see? Near the old steamboat. That's the best fishin' hole for miles. Drop your line over there, Dave."

Dave's reel spun, and his line whined off toward the far end of the steamboat. "I got a fish, Mike!" he called exultantly. "It's your turn."

Inside, listening, Trixie's mind tried desperately to think of a way to attract the boys' attention. What could she do? Her feet were bound. She couldn't stand. Her arms were bound. She couldn't reach for anything. Her mouth was gagged. She couldn't cry out.

Beside her, Honey groaned feebly back in her throat. She was apparently going through the same agony of frustration.

One line whirred and was reeled in. The other boy cast again, and soon Trixie could hear a fish struggling in the water.

Tears gathered in the reddened eyes of the listening girls as minutes, half an hour, then an hour went by. Possible help was so near, yet there was no way to reach out for it.

*If the boys would only come aboard the steamboat!* Trixie thought. If they did, how could she attract their attention? The thumps she made on the floor probably wouldn't be heard outside the door. And the door was locked!

Her eyes darted around the room, from object to object. *I could knock over a chair,* she thought, *if I could bump across the floor to reach it. But it's in that far corner, and the boys would be gone before I could ever reach it.*

Her glance went to the floor, to the debris there.

She singled out the glistening motel key. *Maybe I could push that across the floor and under the door,* she thought. *Then if the boys should come aboard....*

The key was not very far away; it was about half-way between Trixie and the door. But the effort required to reach it made it seem a thousand miles away.

Honey, her eyes following Trixie's to the key, seemed to sense what her friend was trying to accomplish. Her eyes crinkled in encouragement.

Trixie raised her body and wriggled slowly and awkwardly toward the key. She ached in every muscle. As she neared the key, she twisted her body so that she could push it with her chin. Then she lowered her face and pushed. Inch by inch she pushed it. Each convulsive movement of her chin was painful. She was so intent on her efforts, however, that she hardly noticed the pain. Doggedly she prodded till, with one violent thrust, the key disappeared underneath the door.

Then Trixie's head fell back to the floor in triumph. Across the room, Honey's eyes told her that she, too, was rejoicing.

The struggle to push the key had exhausted Trixie. Suddenly a terrible thought flashed through her mind. The boys would probably never see the key! They probably fished here so often that they would have no interest in the hulk of the old steamboat.

They would probably just go on to another fishing hole. They might even go back home, never knowing of the chance they'd had to save the lives of two desperate girls. Tears started in Trixie's eyes.

What was Dave saying to Mike outside?

"Aw, let's quit fishin'. I've got a string now that'll make my ma's eyes pop out."

"Yeah, mine, too," Mike answered. "I didn't stop to think I'll have to clean the fish before Ma cooks 'em."

"I know. Takes all the fun out of it. Say, let's go up on the old boat and drop our lines over the side. Catch some catfish, huh?"

Inside, Trixie listened, holding her breath, waiting for Mike's answer. Would they really come aboard? Would they see the key? Trixie prayed hard.

She heard the boys' feet scrambling up the plank. She heard them running around the lower deck.

*Higher!* Trixie prayed. *Come up higher to drop your lines! Come up to this deck! Come up to this deck and find the key!*

As though in answer to her prayer, she heard Mike and Dave noisily clumping up the stairs that led to the pilothouse.

"Say, look at this!" Mike said, his voice awed. "Someone lost a key. Here, Dave, look!"

"Yeah! It's from a motel in St. Louis." Dave read the inscription. "Gosh, somebody left this since the last time we were here. I never saw it then, did you?"

"Naw. Of course not. Do you suppose they left any other junk inside the pilothouse?"

"We can look."

Mike tried the door and found it locked. "That's funny. It's never been locked before."

Inside, Trixie and Honey, determined to attract the boys' attention, groaned as loudly as their dry, tight throats would let them. Then they raised their bodies and bumped on the floor.

"Did you hear somethin'?" Dave asked.

"Yeah! Do you s'pose there's someone in there?" Mike asked.

Trixie, her body close to the door, bumped hard against it, making it rattle on its old hinges.

"Gosh, didya hear that?" Mike called.

"I sure did. I'm gettin' out of here."

"Me, too!"

Inside, Trixie was desperate. *Try to knock down the door! Try to get to us! Try to untie us!*

Her answer was the sound of running feet. Down the stairs the boys rushed, and across the plank to shore.

Trixie's heart fell to her very toes. She looked at Honey. Honey turned her face away. Then, as a new sound outside intruded, Trixie raised her head again to listen.

"What are you boys up to?" a gruff voice inquired.

"Say, where'd you get that string of bass?"

"Over there near that log," Mike answered. Then he added in an awed voice, "There's someone up there in that old pilothouse!"

"There is?" the man asked. "Now, ain't that somethin'? A body's got a right to go up there if he wants."

"That's not it," Trixie heard Mike insist. "There's someone groanin' up there. We heard 'em. You go up and see."

*Oh, do make him come up to see,* Trixie begged. *Do please, whoever you are, come up here and find us!*

"So someone's groanin' up there, are they?" the man's voice asked. "Who do you think it is, the devil?"

"No, sir, but we found this key."

"That makes you think there's someone up there, does it? Well, let me tell you this. That old steamboat's been there for almost a hundred years, I guess. A body can hear more creakin' an' groanin' in it than you'd hear in a graveyard. What if you did find a key? I've got a collection of junk at home I've picked up that people dropped or threw away here, there, an' everywhere. I'm goin' to fish. You boys go right ahead an' do as you please. If I was you, I'd drop the key in the bushes on your way to the highway. Course, if you want to spend the price of a stamp, you can mail it back to the motel. I wouldn't bother. Now, go on outa here. I don't want any noise disturbin' my fishin'.

I don't think the ghosts up there in the pilothouse are goin' to bother me any."

Hopelessly Trixie heard the boys obey the man's command to run on. The sound of their feet splashing through the swamp grew fainter and fainter, then disappeared.

For a while she heard the man's movements as he cast for bass and reeled in. He sang a folk song of the Mississippi River to himself, in a low, coarse voice. Time went on, and eventually he gathered up his catch and sloshed off down the river's edge.

Trixie bumped her body over close to Honey again. She couldn't bear to look into her friend's eyes. There was nothing left to do but wait . . . wait . . . wait.

The morning sun now shone brightly through the pilothouse windows. Trixie's dry throat longed for a sip of water. Her aching body protested against the strain she had put on it by bumping across the floor . . . a long, futile journey.

It could not be long now till Lontard and his accomplices would return.

Numbly, Trixie and Honey waited, unwanted tears running down their cheeks. There was nothing else they could do.

# Bob-White! • 17

DESPONDENTLY Trixie thought: *Why in the world
did I ever get my hopes up over that key? The only
thing that would help us would be for the boys to take
it to the police. I'm sure they never even thought of
that. Dave and Mike didn't even tell that man who
was fishing that the door to the pilothouse is locked.
If they had, he might have investigated. He'll be just
as sorry as the boys when he finds out he could have
saved our lives.*

As Trixie was thinking, she became aware that
Honey was trying to attract her attention. She raised

her head and saw Honey motion with her eyes toward the shore. The sound of mumbling voices came to her. A coarse laugh. A woman's voice. Someone swore.

Lontard was coming back!

Trixie looked hopelessly into Honey's eyes. *It may be the last time I'll ever see her,* she thought. *It just may be the last time I'll ever see anyone I love....*

Mrs. Aguilera was speaking. "You're making a big mistake if you plan to hurt those girls now."

Her husband answered, "They've gotta be bumped off. There's no other way. We're in so deep now that we've gotta get rid of them. Don't you agree, Frenchy?"

"Keep your mouths shut. I'm the boss of what's going on, and don't you forget it. When I want any opinions, I'll ask for them. Maybe the kids are goners by now. That'd solve some of our problems. Maybe not. I had another plan in mind."

"Like what?" Juan Aguilera asked.

"Like I'll tell you when I get good and ready. Get out of my way. I'll soon know what I've got to do. Let me up those stairs!"

Heavy feet mounted the steps ... nearer ... nearer ... nearer. Then Lontard strode across the space between steps and pilothouse and inserted the key in the lock. Trixie heard a rusty creak as the door yielded. It opened, and Lontard's bulk filled it. The strong morning light shone full on his sneering, wicked face. He grinned maliciously.

"Alive, are you?" He walked across the room and turned the girls over with a prodding foot. "Did you have a pleasant time last night? Did you enjoy a visit from the water rats? They're nice little companions. Aren't you glad to see me?"

Honey hadn't moved since Lontard's heavy foot had touched her. *She's fainted now, I know,* Trixie thought, terror filling her. *Now I'm all alone. Maybe Honey is dead. What is that man saying?*

"Go ahead, Juan, take the gags off!" Lontard ordered. "It surprises you, does it, Elena? You did not know I could be so compassionate? Well, then, do this, too: Give them a drink of water. Quickly!"

Mrs. Aguilera filled a glass from a pitcher on the table. She held it to Trixie's lips. They were so swollen they would hardly open. Trixie shook her head sadly. In a husky voice she said, "Please give Honey a drink first. I think she's fainted. Please try to revive her. Only, if you're going to kill us, don't try. It would be easier for her that way."

Lontard laughed mockingly. "Who said anything about killing such sweet little girls? Untie their arms and legs. Quickly, Juan. Don't look at me that way. I know what I'm doing. Untie them. Don't waste time. I'm merciful and kind. Don't you remember how merciful and kind I can be?"

"If my husband forgets, I remember," Elena

Aguilera said as she soothed Honey's swollen wrists and ankles. "I've watched you with grown people, and I've never said a word. I can't watch you torturing these young people any longer. Try to lift your head, Honey. Take a sip of this water."

Honey's eyes fluttered and opened. Her pale face whitened even more when she saw who was holding her.

"Drink the water, Honey," Trixie said in a low, hoarse voice.

"Yes, drink it!" Lontard commanded. "I'm thinking of taking you on a nice little trip, a sight-seeing jaunt. I don't want you fainting all over the place. Get up! See if you can walk. Juan, lift the little darlings to their dainty feet."

Mrs. Aguilera slowly lifted Honey. The woman stood with her arms sustaining the trembling girl till strength returned to her limbs and she was able to stand alone. Her husband jerked Trixie to her feet roughly. Trixie knew very well that Lontard was not to be trusted, yet they were not going to be killed right away. The thought sent the blood rushing painfully through her numbed legs and hands. She put her arms around Honey. The girls clung to one another.

Lontard dusted his hands together. "There, now, that's better, isn't it? See how kind Pierre Lontard is? How do you repay me? You have committed every known sin against me. You stole my valuable papers. You took them from where I had accidentally left them, in my room. You would not return them to me. You saw me hunting through that wastebasket, and you knew I was hunting for my property. Did you give my property back to me? No."

Trixie and Honey, their arms around one another, did not speak.

"When I went to all the trouble of putting my helpers aboard the *Catfish Princess* to try and recover my papers, did they succeed? No. At that point, Elena was more inclined to help me. She pushed you into the river, Trixie. Everyone would have been sure it was an accident, and, in the excitement, Elena would have had your purse and the papers. But you"—he pointed his long finger at Honey—"had to butt in, and that plot failed.

"Then, that night, you did not give me time to search your stateroom. I had to go overboard, into the water, and swim for shore. I'll never forgive you for that!

"I thought I could take care of things later, but everything went wrong. At every place I'd arranged to meet Bob with his boat, something kept him from stopping. Then I made a bad mistake when the Coast Guard picked up Bob. I should have waited. I'm sure that's the time you turned the papers over to the police. They're bound to have them.

"At every move you frustrated me. And I can't stand frustration! One paper I wanted. Just one paper, more than any other. The map of the river. With it in the hands of the police, our plan is ruined."

"What are you doing all the talking for, Frenchy?" Juan Aguilera interrupted. "You're no history teacher. We know what's already happened. Forget it. What we don't know is what's going to happen."

"A cat has great pleasure playing with a mouse," Lontard growled.

"Meantime, what'll be happening to us?" Juan Aguilera inquired coldly. "We know they handed the papers over to the police. You're getting to the point too slow for me."

"Silence!" Lontard commanded.

"You can't 'silence' me. I'm tired of the way you're carrying on. I'm tired, too, of your chicken-heartedness, Elena. I'll take a few things into my own hands."

Lontard grabbed Aguilera's arm and twisted it till he howled with pain, "I give in! What're you going to do?"

Pierre Lontard turned to the girls. "What I'm going to do is to give you just one more chance to tell me where my property is. Do the police have the papers?"

Neither Trixie nor Honey spoke.

When Lontard spoke again, his voice was as cold as ice. "If you have *not* turned my papers over to the police, and if you will tell me where they are and I can get them back, then I am prepared to set you free. I'll put you on the highway, and in an hour's time you will be with friends again. Did you give them to the police?"

Trixie did not even raise her eyes.

"Will you tell me where they are?" Lontard's voice grew more urgent.

Trixie did not answer. She could not. Even if she had wanted to speak, no sound would have passed her lips, for they were paralyzed with terror.

"Then I must tell you the alternative. I must work fast. Elena does not think little girls should be put in the river. So I will not do that, for her sake." His lips curled.

"That is not your reason," Mrs. Aguilera said. "I fear even more, Pierre Lontard, what you are going to say now."

"You are very perceptive, Elena," Lontard said with frightening sarcasm. "Bodies come to the surface of the river. They do it far too quickly. Fishermen are quick to find them. I cannot take that risk."

"So what?" Juan Aguilera asked. "Make it quick. While we're talking the police are gaining on us. You think they're too dumb to translate those pictures you made on that map. I don't think so. They've got what they call 'cryptographers' in the Secret Service. Maybe you don't know what that is. Maybe that bird who runs *your* country doesn't have 'em. You draw a picture of an old man with a beard in this country, and right away a policeman can tell you it's St. Peter. Same way with all the rest of your artwork."

"There has been no evidence that they know anything of any of our secrets up and down the river," Lontard retorted. "However, it's plain to me that I'll get no cooperation out of these two girls. We'll go from here now."

He grasped Trixie's arm. "Remember the old house where you took refuge in the storm? It's a beautiful old place . . . a rest home. That's where you're going— a nice little ride up the road, then the beautiful old house. You need a long rest, and you'll get it there, both of you."

Trixie clung tightly to Honey. A glimmer of hope arose. Her brothers and Dan and Jim knew of the old house. They *might* hunt for them there. But Lontard's next words brought despair back with a rush.

"We won't be able to give you quarters in the house itself, I'm sorry to say. We need it for our business transactions. Outside the house, down a path, there's a comfortable cave that is well hidden. You will be happy there, I am sure. Of course, we will have to bind you again, arms and feet. A little handkerchief, too, well applied to keep you from making any noise. That's just in case you may be too particular to be satisfied with your quarters."

"For pete's sake, Lontard, quit your lecturing," Juan shouted in disgust. "You may like to listen to the sound of your voice; but I'm sick of it. If you're going to take 'em to the cave, let's take 'em. Want me to tie 'em up first?"

"No!" Lontard cried out. "I'll forget your contemptible remarks and answer them another time. Let them walk. I'll take care of this one." He tightened his hold on Trixie's arm. "You give the other a good strong arm to lean on, Juan. Be a gentleman like me, see?"

Lontard shoved Trixie out of the door and down the steps.

Trembling, their knees shaking and almost crumpling under them, the two girls went with their captors. Trixie knew they were going to certain starvation and death. *No one will ever find us in that cave,* she thought. *If they do, it will be too late. Why, oh why, did I ever get into that car with Mr. and Mrs. Aguilera? Why didn't I wait for the boys? They would have saved me. They always have. Oh, Brian . . . Dan . . . Mart . . . Jim!* Trixie let out a terrified shriek.

Suddenly, miraculously, from the river she heard the shrill whistle of a bobwhite. Then another! And another!

With bursting hearts, the two girls answered: *Bob-white! Bob-white! Bob-white!*

# Reward · 18

PANIC-STRICKEN, Lontard's face reddened in fury. "What goes on here?" he asked, closing his hand over Trixie's mouth. "Don't you dare make a sound again!"

"We're lost!" Mrs. Aguilera cried out. "That whistle is their club signal! We're surrounded!"

On shore a gun cracked. Suddenly the two men released their hold on the captives. With Elena Aguilera following close behind, they ran down the plank—straight into the arms of the police! They were immediately handcuffed and hustled aboard a waiting police boat.

Mr. Wheeler, Mr. Brandio, and the four boys took gentle charge of the two girls. They were so deeply affected that they couldn't say a word. All they seemed to want to do was to touch Trixie and Honey, unbelievably still alive.

"You're safe!" Mr. Wheeler repeated over and over.

For once, words failed Mart.

"We've brought a doctor with us," Mr. Brandio finally said. "Are the girls all right?" he asked the Coast Guard medical officer.

"We're . . . all . . . right, Daddy," Honey said, tears of joy running down her cheeks. "It was awful, though! It was awful, Daddy. I fainted. Trixie was *so* much braver." She collapsed in her father's arms.

"All they did was . . . tie . . . our . . . arms . . . and . . . legs . . . and put gags in our mouths . . . and leave us overnight that way," Trixie said, her voice gaining strength.

"All they did was *what?*" Mart cried.

White-faced, Jim declared in a cold voice, "Killing's far too good for them!"

"Even the electric chair!" Brian added grimly.

"They should get that—at least!" Dan said sternly. "They kidnapped Trixie and Honey."

Trixie, trembling with relief at their miraculous rescue, asked, "How did you know where to look for us, Mr. Wheeler?"

"It's a long story, dear. Right now it must wait. I must be sure neither of you has been permanently harmed. Doctor?" Mr. Wheeler's voice trembled as he waited for the doctor's answer.

"I can see no sign of serious harm," the officer reported. "They are suffering from shock and from the pain of the tight bonds and gags. I'd like to take them to the hospital. Our boat is waiting out there."

"Not a hospital!" Trixie cried. Honey echoed the cry. "All we want, Mr. Wheeler, is to go back to the motel, then take the plane home. I want to see my mom. So does Honey. We thought we'd never see them again in this world."

"We will do as you wish, dear," Mr. Wheeler said gently, tears in his dark eyes. "That is, we will do *almost* as you wish. You must rest for a while in the hospital. Honey fainted, you know. Yesterday morning, you almost drowned. I shall have a difficult time explaining my negligence to your parents, Trixie, and to your mother, Honey. We'll go home just as soon as we possibly can. I wish with all my heart that we had never come here."

Trixie, truly repentant, said quickly, "You don't know how much I wish we never had gone in that car with Mr. and Mrs. Aguilera. You told me to leave it to the police. Can you ever forgive me? It was all my fault and not Honey's at all."

"It was not all your fault," Honey insisted. "You

thought you were doing what the police wanted when Mrs. Aguilera gave you that phony note from Chief Ogilvie. Even then you suspected her. I was so dumb I thought she really liked us. If it's anybody's fault, it's mine."

"Let's not talk about faults right now," Mr. Wheeler insisted. "I'm just so thankful that you two girls are safe. I say it again: I'm sorry I brought you out here."

At that, a listening Coast Guard seaman spoke. His voice was emphatic. "It's a terrible thing that has happened to these girls. They've been frightened cruelly. Think, though, what it will mean to their country!"

"Oh, were those people . . . that Pierre Lontard . . . really trying to steal plans from the airplane factories? Were they, Mr. Brandio?" Trixie asked.

"Here's the answer to that, miss," the seaman answered. "Come over here, and I'll show you!"

The two girls walked haltingly across the deck. The seaman lifted a plank. There, packed as close together as possible, were guns—hundreds of guns!

"Guns?" Trixie asked, awed. "What would anyone who was stealing space secrets want with so many guns?"

Mr. Brandio answered. "This time this trio wasn't after space secrets. It's an even bigger thing you girls have helped to uncover. Those guns were meant to stir up trouble in South America! We believe there are thousands more like them cached up and down the Mississippi River. Those cryptograms will lead to other secret stores."

"Then that map really *was* important?" Trixie asked excitedly.

"Important? It was the most important piece of paper the police have picked up in many years," an officer answered.

"Did that picture of St. Peter on the map really tell you where to find us?" Trixie asked. "Is that what happened? How *did* you save us?"

"The picture helped," the officer answered. "That and some other things."

"As I told you, we'll get to that later," Mr. Wheeler added. "Right now we must go with the doctor. You've both had a shocking experience. Just think, Trixie—that accident in the pool, then . . . I can't bear to think about what followed. Please realize that you must do as the doctor says. You must rest."

"I guess maybe we do need it," Trixie admitted reluctantly. "I'm so thankful to be saved that I can't feel anything else. Honey needs to rest, I know that. I can't honestly believe we're really free—and alive."

Trixie and Honey spent the rest of the day and the night in a beautiful new hospital near the airport. They wanted to go there instead of the Coast Guard base hospital, and the doctor did not object. They shared a double room. Relief at their rescue, exhaustion from their ordeal, and the happy thought that they'd soon be going home again let them sleep the clock around.

When the girls had been taken to their room at the hospital, Jim announced to his father and Mr. Brandio, "The Bob-Whites aren't leaving this hospital. We'll stay right here till the girls leave. If we'd stayed close to them before and hadn't gone to that space exhibit, Trixie and Honey would have been all right."

"I'm staying here, too," Mr. Wheeler said. "I share the blame. I thought the girls would be safe while you were at that exhibit. Most anyone would have thought so . . . locked in their room. They would have been, too, if it hadn't been for Lontard's cunning. He's a desperate man . . . one of the most wanted agents operating in this country. Even though they have him in custody now, my blood runs cold."

So, in spite of Mr. Brandio's suggestions to the contrary and his reassurance that everything possible was being done for the girls, Mr. Wheeler and the boys did not leave. They spent the night in the waiting room. From time to time they napped in the big comfortable chairs, but at the sound of a nurse's or a doctor's footfall, they were instantly on their feet.

The next morning, the girls, Mr. Wheeler, Mr. Brandio, and Chief Ogilvie waited in the lounge at the motel. Bags were packed. At the airfield nearby, a plane, which would return them to New York, was being readied. Mr. Brandio's car stood outside, awaiting word that the plane was prepared.

Trixie's voice broke the silence.

"No one has said one word yet about how you knew where to find us. I couldn't think of a way we could *possibly* be saved. It was awful! After those boys picked up the key, I had a little bit of hope. Even that left when I heard the man who was fishing tell them to throw the key away. What *did* happen, Mr. Wheeler?"

"The boys were a lot smarter than you expected them to be. They took the key to a motel on the highway. They told the manager there about where they had found it and that they thought someone was in the pilothouse. He called the motel here."

"Jeepers!" Trixie's mouth fell open. "Jeepers! Then what happened?"

Chief Ogilvie took up the story. "I can understand why you'd want to keep faith with that boy Lem at Hannibal. . . ."

Trixie's mouth fell open.

"Oh, I knew when I talked to you, Trixie, that something pretty important had happened at Jackson's Island. I could tell that, for some reason, you weren't going to talk about it. So I called one of our men in Hannibal. Lem and Soapy had just been in to tell him about the piece of paper they found. They said one of you told Lem that the paper could be pretty important to the United States. After they'd talked it over, they thought the police should be in on their secret. Of course, the paper *was* important, Trixie. It was the link that we needed in the chain. From it and the cryptograms, it wasn't hard to deduce that the Lontard gang was working south from Hannibal."

"I still don't know what happened after the motel manager called about the key," Trixie interrupted.

"I'm getting to that." Chief Ogilvie smiled. "You see, when you and Honey tried to do things on your own, you interfered with what we were trying to do. We thought we had halted the operation of the Belden-Wheeler Agency, but we sure underestimated Trixie's doggedness."

"Oh, I'm sorry," Trixie said humbly.

"You won't be, when I'm through with my story. As I told you, we were pretty sure the gang led by Lontard was working south. By the way, his name isn't Lontard at all. That's one of his aliases. His real name is Diego Martinez. He encouraged the nickname 'Frenchy' to throw people off. But I'm digressing.

"We had set up headquarters at that highway junction just below St. Peter, and we had channeled all telephone calls and information to our office there. When the manager of this motel relayed the message he had received about the old steamboat, we could act immediately, and we did. You know what happened from then on. The Coast Guard boats were waiting on the river nearby, motors running. In less time than I'm taking to tell you, we were at the old steamboat—and not one minute too soon. Thank heaven for that Bob-White whistle. Its shrillness paralyzed Lontard and the Aguileras till we could get a drop on them with our guns."

"Once again the boys had to rescue us!" Trixie said sadly. "All the Belden-Wheeler Agency did was to slow things down, wasn't it?"

"Not at all! Not at all!" Chief Ogilvie said briskly. "I can't say I'd ever approve of international intrigue and politics as a game for young girls to play, but I'll have to give your agency credit that is due. That stunt of Trixie's, pushing that key under the door, was sheer genius. If you'll forgive a pun, it was the key that unlocked everything—that and your recognition, in the first place, that the papers were significant."

Trixie's blue eyes brightened. She sat up straight, listening.

Honey was all ears, too.

"Yes, sir, the papers you found in your room here were the first tangible clue we had to the operation of this gang. The map, which looked like a child's drawing, was invaluable. Our department had known for a long time that heavy shipments of arms were being sent to countries in this hemisphere where there has been unrest. We couldn't figure where they were being assembled or how they were being shipped. Thanks to the charts, the figures, and the cryptographical map, we have been able to solve a puzzling case."

Trixie looked exultantly at Honey. "Jeepers!"

"Ah, but that isn't all," Chief Ogilvie continued.

"There's more?" Trixie asked excitedly.

"Indeed there is. Lontard, or rather Martinez, really *was* trying to buy an old steamboat. It was an excellent cover for his scheme. He has assembled what probably will prove to be an appalling amount of arms and ammunition at the various places marked on the map. He's used caves, abandoned houses—half a dozen different types of caches. He had expected to load the ammunition on the old steamer and float it to New Orleans, to be shipped from there to insurgent armies. It was a unique method of transportation. I wonder if it would ever have been discovered if it hadn't been for the activity of you two girls. So, you see, we can't be too severe in our criticism of your free-lance operations."

"I still say I'm terribly sorry about all the worry we've caused. I think the United States Secret Service is marvelous. I'm sure it would have turned up the

Martinez gang long before they succeeded in getting that ammunition out of this country."

"That may be," Chief Ogilvie said. "Right now our government isn't too sure that you are right."

Trixie's eyebrows went up, questioning.

"That's true," Chief Ogilvie nodded. "After our investigation is completed, and after an appraisal has been made of the value of the arms that were being smuggled, you may be surprised. You see, the government rewards people who supply information leading to the capture of smugglers. Twenty-five percent of the tax that would have been realized on the smuggled goods will be coming to you girls. How does that sound?"

"It sounds wonderful!" Trixie cried happily. "We'll put it in the Bob-White fund for charity."

"What'll we ever do with that much money?" Honey wondered in a dazed voice.

Mart laughed. "Golly, that won't take too much thinking. We have half a dozen places to put money. There's always the United Nations Children's Fund."

"And CARE," Brian added.

"Red Cross, the United Fund," Dan suggested.

Honey's eyes shone like stars. "Do you know what *I'd* like most of all in the world? I remember pictures of little Vietnamese orphans I saw in a magazine. They were in an ad asking for people to adopt one of them—not really to bring them to this country, but to send money every month to take care of them. Do you possibly think the Bob-Whites could do that?"

"It might cost an awful lot of money," Trixie said dubiously.

"There'll be quite a lot," Chief Ogilvie said. "There'll be enough, I think, to take care of a Vietnamese orphan for *quite* a while."

"Imagine—the Bob-Whites foster parents of a real live baby!" Trixie cried. "Wouldn't it be too perfectly perfect? Do you vote for it?" she asked the boys excitedly.

Dan's hand flew up.

Then Brian's.

And Jim's.

"It's okay with me, just so the orphan's a boy," Mart shouted.

"It doesn't make one bit of difference to me whether it's a boy or a girl," Trixie said dreamily. "I guess we'll take whatever the agency says. It makes this whole trip worthwhile, doesn't it, Honey?"

Honey agreed vigorously.

Just then a messenger came in to inform Mr. Brandio that his plane was ready to take off.

Trixie was the last of the Bob-Whites to thank Chief Ogilvie and to say good-bye. "Now I can go home happy," she said. "This was one of the most exciting trips ever—and I guess we really have something worthwhile to show for it."